THE
LAST
SUMMER
I
LOVED

KATHY WINSLOWER

DEDICATION

For the ones who loved recklessly, lost brutally, and still dared to want more.

CONTENTS

CHAPTER 1: PEDAL TO THE METAL

Juliet "Jules" Montclair

I was almost born in the passenger seat of a Bentley Continental GT, or so the story goes.

My mother, elegant even in labor, refused to give birth in a car like the masses. My father, ever the Montclair, drove her to the private wing of St. Joseph's at 120 miles per hour, his hand clenched around hers, the other wrapped around the wheel. A controlled storm. That was the way of things in our family. Never chaos, never mess. Just precision.

When I was old enough to understand, he told me

I was made for the driver's seat. But what he really meant was: I was made to sit pretty, a Montclair nameplate stamped on my future like a title on a deed.

I didn't want it.

The last week of school was a formality, a grand exit wrapped in designer bows and champagne smiles. St. Rosaline's, where the elite raised their porcelain daughters into cold-blooded powerhouses, was a monument to people like us—Montclairs, Merciers, Langfords. The next generation of power. I sat through the farewell speeches, the hollow laughter, the whispered gossip in the hallways that reeked of privilege and Prada.

I played my part. Crossed my legs. Smiled at the right people.

And suffocated.

Because where I came from, girls like me didn't get to be reckless. Girls like me didn't get to want. Not without consequences.

Montclair daughters didn't chase boys, didn't let anyone get too close, didn't risk scandal or ruin. Our names were investments. Our lives, carefully curated.

But I knew what happened to girls who did. I'd

seen the wrath of my father, sharp as a blade and just as merciless.

I could already hear my father's voice ringing in my head. *This is your future, Juliet. Don't fight what's already decided.*

The thing about fathers like mine? They don't expect rebellion. They expect obedience wrapped in a silk bow. They expect their daughters to marry well, manage empires, and smile in the faces of men who mistake their spine for softness.

He expected me to fall in line. He expected me to be his perfect Montclair heir. What he didn't expect was this:

By midnight, I'd be gripping the wheel of a car he would never approve of, tearing through Toronto's underground racing circuit like the daughter he never saw coming.

The Montclair estate was a palace of cold glass and marble, hard edges and vacant rooms. It had the scent of wood polish and cash, and on evenings such as these, it seemed more like a mausoleum than a house. Dinner was as always—silent, aside from the deliberate scrape of silver against fine plates.

Victor Montclair presided at the head of the table, a monarch with empire laid out before him. I sat across from him, spine straight, a daughter raised to be seen, not heard.

"The Langford family will join us for dinner next Friday," he said, voice clipped, efficient. "You will attend."

I didn't answer right away. I lifted my glass, took a sip of something expensive. The silence stretched between us like a taut wire.

"Are you asking or telling me?"

A muscle in his jaw ticked. "This is not up for discussion."

Of course, it wasn't. Nothing ever was.

Dominic Langford was exactly the kind of boy my father approved of—old money, good manners, a future made of golden handshakes and power plays. We had exchanged a grand total of twenty words in our lifetime, none of which had been worth remembering.

My father didn't care about that. He cared about dynasties. About alliances. About making sure Montclair & Motors remained untouchable.

I tapped my fork against my plate. "And if I have

other plans?"

His gaze cut through me like winter air. "Cancel them."

I met his stare with a slow, deliberate smile. "I'll think about it."

A lie. Because in four hours, I'd be breaking every single one of his rules.

At exactly eleven-thirty, I was moving through the garage, fingers ghosting over the hood of a machine built in secret.

The car wasn't just a car. It was a rebellion crafted in chrome and steel. A sleek, black Porsche 911 Carrera, gutted and rebuilt with hands that shouldn't have known how to do it. Hands that had spent years in the Montclair garages when no one was looking, learning what it meant to take something apart and make it better. Faster. Stronger.

No one knew about this car. No one knew about the nights I spent with grease under my nails and the smell of oil thick in my hair. No one knew that this was the only thing that made me feel real.

The garage wasn't part of the pristine Montclair estate my father paraded to investors. It was an old service bay, abandoned and forgotten at the edge of the property. The kind of place no one checked because it wasn't glamorous enough to matter. But to me, it was a kingdom built in secret, a sanctuary where the expectations and legacy pressing against my throat couldn't reach me.

I ran my fingers over the Porsche's hood, my reflection warped and slick beneath the dim light. "You ready for this, baby?" I murmured, circling to pop the hood. The engine was a thing of beauty—modified, recalibrated, refined beyond anything stock. I had spent months on this—sourcing the right parts, tuning it down to the millisecond, making sure it could outrun anything that came for it. Or for me.

I pulled out my phone, fingers smudged with oil as I swiped the screen. The notification was waiting.

New Entry Slot Open – Midnight Run Toronto. Register Now.

Unlike the old days, this wasn't some back-alley deal with cash exchanged under neon lights. No whispered passwords or waiting for a man with a clipboard. Everything was digital now—encrypted, anonymous. The system ran on an AI algorithm that matched racers the moment they checked in.

I exhaled slowly and tapped the confirmation.

Registered. Await match at check-in.

A thrill skated down my spine, sharp and electric. My first race. The thought curled hot in my chest, a perfect storm of fear and anticipation. I could only hope I wouldn't wreck before I even had the chance to prove myself.

I reached for the mask tucked inside the glove compartment. Black, sleek, designed to shield my identity just enough. If my father ever found out, he'd lock me in that glass house of his and throw away the key.

I pulled the mask over my face, adjusting the edges. In the mirror, my reflection was something else entirely—sharper, untouchable. No longer Jules Montclair, heir to a legacy she didn't want.

I was just a driver now.

I swung into the driver's seat, heart thudding against my ribs. The second my fingers curled around the wheel, something inside me unlocked.

This was mine. This moment. This machine. This night.

With a deep breath, I started the engine.

The roar shattered the silence, and I smiled.

The streets of Toronto were alive with the kind of electricity that only came out at night. The kind that hummed in your bones, that sent adrenaline licking up your spine. I pulled into the lot just past the industrial docks, where the underground racing circuit pulsed under flickering streetlights and the scent of burnt rubber and gasoline.

Engines revved like war drums. Neon lights reflected in oil-slick puddles, throwing distorted ghosts of the racers onto the pavement. People leaned against their cars, laughter sharp as shattered glass, the air thick with money, risk, and something unnamable. This wasn't the world of Montclairs and Langfords, of carefully curated futures and sterile wealth. This was raw, reckless hunger—people chasing the rush of speed the way others chased power.

Tonight, I was one of them.

The mask was warm against my skin, concealing my face, my identity. No one knew who I was beneath the black carbon fiber shell, just another anonymous racer with something to prove. My entry had been easy—too easy. A burner phone, a shadow account, a few well-placed bribes, and suddenly, Juliet Montclair no longer existed.

In her place, there was *Nyx*.

A name ripped from old poetry. The kind of name that would outlive me if I let it.

I rolled forward, fingers flexing over the wheel, feeling the low, guttural purr of my car like a living thing beneath me. And then I saw him.

Not a racer. A spectator. A lad who did not belong to this world but stood in it as if he owned the night.

He was leaning against the rim of the crowd, apart but not aloof, the swaying light of a streetlamp nearby slicing deep shadows across his face. Dark eyes, impenetrable, fixed on the scene as if he were analyzing it, weighing. There was a focus in the way he stood, motionless but not inactive, his hands curled in the pockets of his leather jacket as if he had nothing to prove and everything to lose.

My stomach flipped. Irritation, maybe. Or something worse.

I shouldn't have noticed him. I shouldn't have felt the moment stretch, the static between us snapping like a live wire. I didn't know his name, didn't know why he stood out in a sea of people who were louder, flashier, more desperate to be seen.

But I knew I would remember him.

And then, there was *him*.

Tyson "Ty" Vega.

Not leaning—*lounging*—against his Dodge Challenger like the world was made for him to own. Dark eyes catching the low glow of the streetlights, watching, waiting. A storm waiting to break.

He didn't know it was me, his cousin. Couldn't have known. Not beneath the mask, not in the darkness. But he saw the car, saw the way I handled it, and something in his expression sharpened.

Ty wasn't just a hothead, not just a street king with a reputation carved in burnt rubber and broken bones. He was worse. He was a predator wrapped in wealth, a self-made executioner who enforced the Montclair name with blood and fire. And if he ever found out who was behind the wheel of this car, behind *this* mask—

I couldn't let that happen.

Our eyes met across the lot, and something inside

me tightened, coiled, *snapped.*

I didn't flinch. I didn't look away.

The starting light flickered overhead, counting down to chaos.

I gripped the wheel, foot hovering over the gas. The boy in the crowd. Ty's watchful stare. The weight of expectation curling around my throat like a noose.

I was prepared to let it all burn.

xoxoxo

CHAPTER 2: THE ONE THAT GOT AWAY

Romeo "Romy" Cruzer

I never planned to stay in this life forever. That's what I told myself, anyway.

Each time I wiped grease from my hands in the rear of my father's auto shop, each time I heard him speak of the business as if it were a legacy rather than a curse, each time I saw Marco roll his eyes and mutter about there being no way out—I told myself that I was different.

But the reality was, the longer you were there, the

more difficult it was to leave. The gravity of the Cruzer name seeped into your bones, heavy as oil and just as impossible to scrub away. My father didn't even ask if I wanted to inherit. He assumed. Like a car coming off the assembly line, predestined and unalterable.

And perhaps once, when I was young and stupid enough to believe I had a decision, I believed I could escape it. Believed if I drove fast enough, worked hard enough, I could make something of myself without the specter of hotwired cars and hissed threats following me.

Then reality cut in.

I quit school. Wanted to say something to my parents—thought about it more times than I can remember. But whenever I pictured it, I saw my mother's face fold up, heard the sound of her voice breaking when she asked what she did wrong. I saw my father's silence, the hard, weighty kind that was a disappointment greater than yelling could ever be. And then, finally, I knew precisely how it would play out.

He'd just look at me for a long time, then give me a wrench and tell me to get back to work.

For the past two weeks, I maintained the charade.

Arose each morning as if I had a place to be. Picked up my backpack, exited out the front door, and acted as if I was going to class. I'd cruise around for a while, get coffee, park in a lot, and wait for long enough to let enough time go by before looping back around to the shop.

My cousin, Marco found it absolutely hilarious.

"Yeah, you really believe they're not gonna figure it out?" He leaned against a workbench, arms folded, observing me replace an air filter in a Civic that wasn't exactly legally obtained. "Your old man's not dumb."

I blew out through my nose, eyes on the task at hand. "I know."

"You have, what? A day? Maybe two before someone rats or he catches you sneaking back here too soon?"

I over-tightened a bolt with too much force. "I'll make it work."

Marco chuckled to himself, shaking his head. "Yeah? So what's the strategy then, genius?"

I had no reply.

Dinner was the worst part. Sitting at the dinner table, acting as if I had a typical day, nodding along when my mom asked about school.

"Did you hand in that history paper?" she asked one evening, shoving a plate of arroz con pollo in front of me.

I nodded. Lied. "Yeah."

"And your grades?"

I shrugged. "Fine."

She examined me for a long moment, lips compressing, but didn't push.

My dad hardly glanced up from his plate. "Doesn't matter. Kid's got a real education waiting for him in the shop."

My Mom sighed, shaking her head. "Raul—"

"He's gonna take over one day," my dad said, spearing his food with his fork. "Might as well start now."

My mom glanced at me like she was thinking of saying something else. Maybe she did know. Maybe she could already tell I was lying. But she just turned back to her plate, silent in a way that made my stomach knot.

I wanted to tell her the truth. Wanted to confess that I wasn't sitting in some classroom, that I was deceiving both of them every day. But the words jammed somewhere between my ribs, pushed between pride and shame and the burden of my last name.

So I remained silent.

And the lie grew broader.

Marco was the only one who wasn't shocked.

You're in deep now, hermano," he told me, slapping my back as I tightened bolts on a stripped Camaro. He was always saying things in advisories I never heeded. "Once you're in, you don't get to leave."

I was going to leave. Make something of it. Something my own.

Because I wasn't him. I wasn't irresponsible. I wasn't seeking trouble.

Trouble still found me anyway.

It arrived in the excuse of an illegal race— one I had no business being at. One I told myself I'd just watch, keep my hands clean, stay out of the mess. Like that had ever worked before.

The parking lot behind the factory docks was filled when we drove up, the stench of gasoline and sweat hanging heavy, the electric snap of excitement crackling like pre-storm static. Engines growled in the distance, headlights slicing through cracked asphalt.

Home. Horribly so.

"Five minutes," Marco grumbled, looking down at his phone. "We do a recon, then we bounce."

And then she appeared.

The minute the car came rolling in, all else dissipated. Black Porsche 911 Carrera, low and deadly, its motor purring like a knife stropped on whetstone. Customized work to the nth screw—adjusted aerodynamics, carbon-fiber trim, an engine so slick it was verging on the surgical.

"Hell's bells," Marco said. "Is she one of yours?"

I didn't respond, because I didn't know. But for some reason, I couldn't help staring at her. And by her- I mean the car.

I knew all the racers worth knowing in this city. All the cars that had made their mark. But I'd never seen this one before.

And when the driver emerged, fitting her gloves as though she had nothing better to do with her time, I knew—whoever she was, she wasn't here to mess around.

She was here to win.

Marco whistled low. "She is new."

"Yeah." I remained neutral in my tone, but my thoughts were already racing, already trying to think of every name I knew, every single racer in the circuit. She wasn't one of them.

Everything she did was intentional, planned. She wasn't like the others—wasn't primping or flaunting. Just quiet confidence, the kind that made people clam up and listen.

Whoever she was, she knew how to play the game.

Marco whistled softly. "Think she's got the guts to run?"

I breathed out, my fingers tightening on the frayed leather of my jacket.

"I believe she's going to shake things up."

The masked driver shifted, barely enough for the neon to reflect off the sharp angle of her jawline, the edge of a smile under the mask.

And in that instant, I knew.

Whoever she was, she wasn't just another newbie driver.

The lineup at the corner of the industrial lot, the smell of burned rubber and gas heavy in the air. A group of onlookers surrounded them, their chatter filled with excitement. This was the sort of race that people would be discussing for weeks—the sort where legends were made or lost.

Tyson "Ty" Vega was behind the wheel of his black and gold Dodge Challenger, fingers tapping against the steering wheel as if he was already in victory mode. He'd dominated these streets for years. Unbeatable, untouchable. The type of guy who looked at people like me and saw a pest. The type of guy who looked at the girl in the black Porsche and saw a joke.

He stuck his head out the window, showing the sort of smirk that got my knuckles tingling. "Nice wheels, princess. Did Daddy get it for ya?"

The girl didn't move. Didn't even glance at him. Simply readjusted the gloves on her hands, her back as relaxed as if she'd performed this stunt a thousand times already.

Ty laughed. "Not much of a chatterbox, eh? That's fine. You can hold your breath until you tell me how you lost."

Still nothing. Only the slow, deliberate motion of her fingers closing around the wheel, tightening infinitesimally.

Marco edged closer, his voice low. "She has a death wish."

"Perhaps," I breathed, eyes on the Porsche. "Or perhaps she's just better than Ty is."

The girl finally shifted her head just so, looking toward Ty. No word. Merely a fleeting, knowing smirk under that mask—barely perceptible, but enough to create a shock wave through the crowd.

Ty's face shadowed. "Okay, honey. Because you're new here, I'm going to make you a special offer. Don't blink. And don't cry when you lose."

She cocked her head, finally breaking her silence. "You talk a lot. Guess we'll see if you drive as good as you run your mouth."

A couple of people laughed. Not many. Just enough to make Ty's hands grip the wheel tighter.

Then she faced the road again, unruffled.

Someone shouted, "Yo, what do we call you, new girl?"

For a moment, I didn't think she'd respond. But then she reached up, adjusting the strap of her mask.

"Nyx."

Nyx. A name that was short and sharp as a blade

cutting through the darkness. The Greek goddess of night—appropriate for someone who moved like a shadow, like she didn't exist at all.

Marco whistled softly. "Damn. Dramatic much?"

I didn't respond. Because there was something in the way she said it. Like she wasn't selecting the name—like it had already been hers for a long, long time.

The starter lifted his hand. The countdown started.

Three.

The engines growled, alive and famished. My heartbeat throbbed in time with the vibrating earth.

Two.

Ty cracked his neck, eyes fixed straight ahead. If he was tense, he didn't show it.

Nyx simply sat there, rigid as stone, fingers curling once over the wheel.

One.

I breathed out. Marco leaned forward, voice hardly a whisper. "This is gonna be fun."

The flag dropped.

xoxoxo

CHAPTER 3: RISKY BUSINESS

Juliet "Jules" Montclair

The air was heavy with gasoline and heat, the crowd a living, breathing entity on the boundary of the track. Headlights cut through the blackness, casting raw streaks of white across the broken road. This was my world—the only place I ever felt like I belonged.

My hold clamped over the wheel, fingers curled up within my gloves. The mask hid most of my face, but my eyes were left uncovered, keen and acute. No helmet. A mere skin of material separating me from the truth Tyson Vega would never understand.

Ty's car rumbled along with me, loud and brutish, a monster forged to overwhelm through pure strength. He was self-assured—negligent, even. He believed this already belonged to him. But that was his initial error.

His second mistake was believing that I was simply another newbie racer.

I breathed out slowly as the flag girl advanced, lifting her arm. My heartbeat was calm, in rhythm with the low, ravenous growl of my car. Ty gave his engine a second rev, arrogant. The crowd moved forward, on edge, salivating for the type of anarchy that only a race like this could provide.

And then, him.

Standing just at the starting line, arms folded, eyes unreadable. The handsome guy I'd clocked before, the one who didn't simply watch—he observed. Calculating. Analyzing. I should've averted my eyes, but I didn't. There was something about his stance, like he was anticipating something to occur.

The flag fell.

I stomped on the accelerator.

The world blurred.

The vehicle shot forward, unbridled power

propelling Ty in the first couple of seconds. Predictable. He was driving on horsepower and ego, goosing his vehicle like it was invincible. But I wasn't concerned. Races weren't lost at the beginning—races were lost at the point where your opponent knew they had already lost.

Ty dove into the first turn, hard and fast. Too hard. The weight of his car pushed him wide. I remained tight, my car clinging to the inside curve, traction control gluing me onto the road as if I'd been sewn into the pavement. Smooth. Seamless. Accuracy over brute force.

I could hear Ty's anger in the rum of his engine as he stood it on its end down the next straight. His car pulled ahead again, but I had him timed now. His car was pure brute power, no skill. He was attempting to scare me, but I wasn't the one holding my wheel too hard.

Halfway down the track, he was still leading us. But only for a little while.

I threw a switch.

The turbocharged engine growled back in an instant, torque hitting me like a boxer's punch in the chest. My Porsche catapulted forward, a silver needle cutting through air between us.

Ty's face jerked to mine. Not soon enough.

I nudged by him, a breath between street and steel. Ty screamed past me, but I was in the last few yards already. He floored it in rage, the harsh rumble of his engine rattling the road.

I flipped the last switch.

Active aerodynamics took over, compensating my speed, holding me glued to the road as if wings were sewn into my tires. Ty pushed harder, but power with no control was a recipe for disaster.

I soared across the finish line first.

Silence.

And then—madness.

The audience exploded, a wave of cheers and shouts, the rapid-fire chatter of bets being cashed in back-alley deals. I hardly heard any of that. My heart was the louder sound, pounding in my ears, shaking through my bones. The kind of rush that didn't wear off readily.

Ty pounded his fist on the wheel, a crisp, metallic sound that sent a shiver through the crowd. Someone whistled softly. His expression contorted with rage, all clenched jaw and white-knuckled fists.

I could've sneered. Could've rubbed it in his face. But I didn't have to. The truth was already printed on the way he wouldn't meet my eyes, the way his chest heaved and fell too quickly, the way his pride was in shambles at my feet.

I got out of my Porsche, mask firmly in position, hands not shaking. Control was the key. Control was what separated winning and losing, survival and destruction.

And then—him.

I saw the flash of movement before I caught sight of him, as if the air itself shifted. The handsome one. He was staring at me, standing just at the edge of the crowd, arms relaxed at his sides, head cocked. As if he was entertained. As if he was curious.

As if he noticed something that others did not.

I ignored him. Or at least attempted to. I stripped off my gloves, curling my fingers into the night air. But when I stepped, he stepped. When I breathed out, he edged closer.

"You've got mad skills, chica," he said. His voice

was smooth, with an edge of interest. Calculated, but not cold. "Didn't think anyone could take Tyson Vega down like that."

"He was sloppy," I said, nonchalant. I was excellent at nonchalant.

His smile was slow, deliberate. "You always this cocky, or just when you're wearing a mask?"

I shrugged, letting the adrenaline drop. "Wouldn't you like to know."

The way he regarded me then—sharp, assessing, like he was stripping away layers just by standing there—made something strange slither down my spine.

He laughed. Warm. Surprising.

"Name's Romy."

I didn't offer mine. Not yet. Names carried weight. Names carried consequences.

"Nyx," I said instead.

Romy repeated it, rolling the syllables on his tongue, testing for truth. He didn't think I was serious. I could tell by the flash of his eyes, the way he rolled the name on his tongue, as if waiting for me to set him straight.

"Race me next time."

Challenge, not a request.

I was about to open my mouth with another biting retort when the sirens began.

As dominoes, the crowd changed. An instant of calm—chaos. Flesh hit motion, shadows stripping themselves from the sides of the alleys, fists wrapping around bills before shoving it into their jackets. Motors fired up once more, the urgent cries covered. Brakes shrieked.

Run.

Romy cursed under his breath. Controlled. As if he were already mapping his next strategy.

I didn't wait to see what it was.

I moved.

Quick.

Dove into my Porsche, hands firm as I shifted into gear. I was already peeling out of the parking lot before the first set of flashing red and blue lights divided the night in two.

This was the part that made or broke you. The real race after the race. The part where speed wasn't so much about winning—it was about not getting caught.

A black Mustang came blazing into my rearview.

I nearly laughed.

Nice try, Romy.

He was staying with me, pace for pace, turn for turn, and that was good—but not good enough. Not nearly.

I weaved through two lanes, passing between cars that were creeping along, city lights dissolving into neon slashes. My heartbeat was in time with the engine, a deep thrum in my side. Each second, each hard draw of air, each precisely measured slipstream was a defiance of the prison of my existence.

I sped up the next turn too aggressively. Intentionally.

A test.

Romy trailed along.

Interesting.

I clenched my teeth, accelerating. If he thought he could tail me, he was going to discover the world of difference between driving and racing.

I weaved through an intersection just in time as the light turned red. Romy paused—a split second, but it counted.

Counted enough for me to vanish.

I continued to drive, feeding off the high of adrenaline until the city smoothed out into the familiar. Houses with gates. Chilly marble driveways. Wealth that preceded obligations I'd never requested.

It wasn't until I eased my car up the long arc of my parents' estate that my heart relaxed and my hands stilled on the steering wheel. The presence of the night stayed with me, tracing along my skin.

I shut down the engine. Sat there for a moment, looking at my own face reflected in the windshield.

Pulled off my gloves.

Pulled off my mask.

The girl who emerged from the Porsche wasn't the one who'd just dropped Tyson Vega in the dust.

She was Juliet Montclair. Groomed. Composed. A name with a weight too great to bear.

I hurried back towards the mansion, climbed the stairs, sliding into the side door. I was back home like I had never left. The security system flashed green. Quiet approval. A fresh start.

The air inside was still, untouched. No smell of burnt asphalt, no zappy rush of velocity in the walls.

Simply cold marble, pricey quiet, and the old familiar pressure pinching down against my ribs.

I went up the stairs, quietly, carefully, though I didn't have to. My father was a creature of habit—at this time of night, he was either in his study, reading files full of legal jargon, or in the living room, soaking up the news like it was scripture.

My room was just as I had left it. Spotless. Unscathed. An ideal deception.

I raked my hand through my hair, shaking it loose of its tidy setup. Tugged on the edge of my hoodie, wrinkling it just so. The smell of adrenaline and gas still on my skin, so I yanked it off, letting the cold air nibble at my arms. The mirror reflected my image—a girl with rosy cheeks and crazed eyes, flying high off the night.

I had to stifle it.

I pulled the blankets back on my bed, bunched up the sheets into haphazard knots, tossed my shoes into the closet. It needed to be lived in. It needed to appear that I had always been here.

I waited. Timing out the seconds. When the moment felt perfect, I walked out into the hallway.

Below, the TV glowed, the muted murmur of

sounds seeping into the silence. I knew before I even touched the landing what it would be.

"…an epidemic of illegal street racing. The mayor's office assured immediate action…"

The news reader's tone was polished, practiced, but underlying it was a hint of hardness—a glint of barely muted disapproval.

My father stood before the screen, jaw clenched, hands clasped, behind his back. His face was chiseled from years of diet and workout, hard and unyielding, his eyes locked on the grainy video rolling along on the screen, his expression unmoving.

A car—my car—gliding through the darkness like a ghost.

"This city is an outrage," he growled, his tone like the fall of a gavel. "And I want to know why the Mayor won't do anything about it."

I swallowed hard, the words weighing in my chest like lead.

- Keep your face neutral. Keep your voice calm.

"Everything all right?" I asked, entering the room as if I wasn't suffocating on the smell of charred rubber and streetlight darkness.

He turned, and for a fleeting moment, the hardness in his face relaxed. "Nothing you need to worry about, sweetheart."

Sweetheart. As if I were something fragile. Something that needed to be shielded.

I nodded, pushing my lips into something easy, something neutral. "Alright."

His eyes rested on me for a second, his face searching for something—cracks, perhaps. Weakness. I didn't give him anything.

I turned before the heaviness of it could press down any further, before the buzz of the news could burrow under my skin.

Inside, I closed my bedroom door, pushing myself back against it, my pulse still pounding in my throat.

One day, I wouldn't have to wear the mask.

One day, I'd drive as Juliet Montclair.

And the world would have to catch up.

For the first time in a long time, I felt alive.

xoxoxo

Chapter 4: No Strings Attached

Romeo "Romy" Cruzer

I wasn't meant to be here. Not again.

Not on this side of town, not at another race, not running after a girl whose face I hadn't even seen. But I was.

The parking lot of the warehouse was filled—engines humming, neon under the hood of too-fast cars, too-loud mouths. Money changed hands as if it was nothing, as if people didn't die for it. Burnt rubber and gasoline filled the air, the thud of bass-pounding music resonating through my chest. This was a world built on risk, on high-stakes and wild gambles, and tonight I was all in.

I navigated the crowd, paying no mind to the shouts of guys attempting to sell me on their next big race, their next big score. I was not here for them.

I was here for her.

And then I spotted her.

Not driving this time. No Porsche sleek at her fingertips, no rush of speed enveloping her completely. Just her—dark hoodie, mask still in place, standing at the lot's edge as if she waited for something.

For me.

I moved forward, my step slow and measured. "Nyx."

She shifted her head to the side, as if acknowledging without making the effort obvious. "Sorry, do I know you?"

I grinned. "C'mon. Don't act stupid. The last I heard, you were stalking me on the highway."

She folded her arms, mask concealing what expression may have crossed her face. "You're mistaken. I don't stalk people. They stalk me."

Cocky. I approved.

I moved a step closer, close enough that I could pick up the whiff of gasoline and something sweet— vanilla? Possibly something tangier, like citrus. My voice fell just so that she would have to really hear me.

"Romeo Cruzer," I told her, presenting my name like a risk, like a challenge. "But everyone calls me Romy."

Something in how she stood changed, the angle of her head, the tightness of her shoulders. Then—

"Cruzer?" she said again, as if the name felt off in her mouth. "As in—"

I interrupted her before she could get out the rest. "Yeah. Cruzer Auto & Body. The place on Dundas." I stared at her, hoping for recognition, for something to fall through. "You ever need work done, stop by. I'll personally tune your car myself."

A smile crept at the corners of her mask. "I'm good. I tune my own car."

My smile grew. "Independent. I approve.

She laughed, shaking her head, but didn't step back when I shut the final of the distance between us.

"You only race on special occasions, or are you

just afraid tonight?" I inquired, tone tinged with challenge.

Her head canted slightly, a smile I couldn't see spreading beneath that mask. "If I were afraid, would I be standing right here?"

Good point.

I pointed to her mask. "You gonna let me see your face, or is this some Phantom of the Opera shit?"

She snorted a laugh, a low, stinging sound. "You want to see my face?"

I stared back at her, unblinking. "Yeah."

She weighed it. Or pretended to, before she leaned forward, voice falling just for me. "I need you to do something for me.

I raised an eyebrow. "That so?"

She gestured toward the eastern part of the city, where Montclair & Motors loomed like a temple to the wealthy. "There's an antique item at the Montclair showroom. Fetch it, and I'll show you my face."

I let out a laugh. "You have a death wish? That joint is infested with security. Traps galore."

Nyx leaned her head to one side, her voice almost purring as she spoke again. "Aw... are you a scared little baby?"

I laughed. "You're really pressing my ego now."

She shrugged. "If it gets me what I want, I'll press all the time."

I watched her, trying to determine what she was playing at. I knew she was fibbing about something. About why she needed that antique, how she even knew it existed. But I didn't care.

I enjoyed the game.

I enjoyed her.

And I enjoyed the way her voice curled around a dare like silk and steel combined.

"Done," I said, offering my hand.

She shook it, her hand firm, assertive. "Don't get caught, Romeo."

She spoke my name as if it were a warning. As if she already understood that this was the beginning of something we could no longer control.

I knew it too.

But I didn't care.

And then I did it.

Breaking into Montclair & Motors wasn't the most difficult thing I'd ever done, but it wasn't a stroll in the park, either. The building was a fortress—cameras, motion detectors, pressure plates. The kind of security designed to keep guys like me out.

But I was good.

Better than good, really. I ghosted through that dealership and didn't set off a single alarm, not a single flashing red light, not so much as a whisper of movement to alert people. My own personal performance left me in awe. Slick. Neat. A goddamn work of art. And then I stood before the display case, gazing at the antique stopwatch perched prettily under glass as if it were some sort of sacred artifact, and I came close to laughing. This thing? This is what she desired?

I didn't spend any time wondering about it. Pulled the lock, grabbed the stopwatch, and slipped out where I came in—no sirens, no alarms, no issues. Before my boots struck the pavement two blocks away, I could hear the hum of the security system still going on, none the wiser that it had been fooled.

She waited on the roof like she'd promised, arms crossed, dark hoodie zipped up tight around her body. Still masked. Still enigma.

I threw the stopwatch to her. "Satisfied?"

She caught it one-handed, palm-flicking it back and forth. "Not bad.

Not bad? I put my ass on the line for this, and she gives me not bad? I inched closer, slow and deliberate, closing the distance between us. "I want my reward."

She tilted her head. "I said I'd show you my face."

I shook my head. "Not good enough. You didn't warn me how difficult the challenge was gonna be. That's just mean. That means I get to raise my price."

A silence. Silence taut between us. The city sounds muffled beneath it—the distant honk of a cab, the thump of bass from a club a few blocks away, the wind slicing sharp through the skyscrapers.

"What do you want?" she said, her voice level. But I detected the hitch in it. A strand of something unsaid.

"A kiss."

That stopped her.

Not nastily. More like I'd pushed her off course for half a second. Like she hadn't had time to duck.

She breathed softly. Then—"One condition."

I smiled. "Tell me."

"You keep your eyes closed."

I didn't even think. Grinning, I closed my eyes. "Deal.

For an instant, nothing. Just the wind on my skin, the whiff of her—something thin, metallic, a blend of gasoline and something sweeter below. Then the distance between us vanished.

Her fingers stroked my jawline first, the lightest of touches, drawing a path down my cheek. Slow. Cautious. Charting me out as if I was something to memorize. I could sense her breath before I could feel it, heat against my skin, a temptation at first, a test. Then her lips were against mine—gentle at first, a bare whisper of touch before she angled her head and deepened.

Heat coursed through me, a fire in my blood intensifying the kiss until it was no longer a kiss. It was a collision, a crash. Something neither of us had intended but neither of us could prevent. I moved in, hands to her waist, drawing her toward me. She didn't move away. She dissolved into me, hands tracing into my hair, nails scraping lightly at the base of my neck. The kiss was drawn out, measured—like we had all the time in the world and none whatsoever.

I felt her. The contours of her face under my hands. The curve of the jaw, the gentle slope of the cheekbones, the slight shiver that ran through her when I outlined my thumb on her chin.

I could feel her artificial nails pressing into the back of my head, but where our mouths touched, she was real. No barriers. No secrets. Just this.

I wanted more.

I didn't know how long it lasted—seconds, minutes, a lifetime packed into a stolen moment—but when she withdrew, I kept my eyes closed.

Then, hardly a whisper—"Open them."

I did.

And I swore the world slowed down.

She was—God. She was stunning. heartbreakingly beautiful. Not the way glossy magazines published beauty, not the way girls strutted around as if they were entitled to the world The face that could break a guy in all the best and worst ways. Dark eyes surrounded by thick lashes, full lips still parted slightly as if she wasn't finished kissing me.

She was dangerous.

She was gazing at me as if she already regretted

showing me.

But whatever was in her face—something wary, uncertain—made my heart pound harder than the kiss did.

"Your name?" I said, voice grittier than I meant it to be. "Your real name?"

She paused. Barely a beat, but I saw it.

Then—"Jules."

And before I could speak again, before I could cling to the moment, she disappeared.

I didn't pursue her.

Didn't have to.

She was already in my mind, scorching a trail through me like a burning fuse.

I tried hard not to think about her.

Failed badly.

Jules was lodged in my brain like a tune I couldn't shut off. The way she moved, the way she spoke, the way she kissed me like she was both surrendering and resisting simultaneously. She was wildfire in mystery, and I was already scarred.

I just couldn't get her out of my head.

Jules.

I relived last night a hundred times, the feel of her lips, the sound of her name spoken as a secret. I was so immersed in it I didn't even notice Marco, my cousin, until he slapped me on the head. "Jesus, Romy. You look like you were hit by a truck."

I pushed him away. "Screw off."

Marco chuckled. "You're thinking about a girl."

"No, I'm not."

"Liar. Who is she?"

"None of your business."

His smile grew. "Damn. First kiss?"

I didn't respond.

Marco chuckled. "Oh, man. You're so screwed."

Perhaps I was.

I didn't care.

But Marco, didn't let it slide. He clocked me zoning out and latched onto it like a damn leech. "You're still thinking about that girl, huh?" he said, lounging on the hood of my car, smirking. "Damn, Romy, what'd she do? Whisper sweet nothings about fuel injection in your ear?"

"Shut up, man."

Oh, so it's serious, huh." He whistled softly.

"Took you long enough to get your first kiss. Was she worth the wait at least?"

I tossed a rag at him. He dodged it, chuckling. "Touchy, touchy."

And the TV in the corner of the shop caught my eye. The news was on—some press conference, city politics crap. But the name Montclair made me turn my head.

Victor Montclair remained at the podium, all glittering conceit in a sharp suit. The caption ran along the bottom: MAYOR DECLARS CITYWIDE CRACKDOWN ON UNSANCTIONED AUTO BUSINESSES.

I felt my stomach knot.

This wasn't a typical headline. This was targeted at us—at my world, my dad's shop, our whole stupid world. My attention had caught the news report, but what made my stomach plummet was who was talking.

Victor Montclair.

Then I saw her.

"It's her."

Standing beside Victor Montclair, dressed in a baby-pink suit and skirt, not resembling in the least the girl who had kissed me on that roof.

I stood there, stunned, the wind sucked from my lungs.

Jules wasn't only a girl who drove.

She was Juliet Montclair.

Marco whistled low, shaking his head. "Well, well," he drawled. "Guess your mystery girl has a last name."

Montclair.

I took the full impact of it like a head-on crash. She's his daughter.

Daughter of the man who was trying to destroy my family.

Off-limits.

Jules wasn't just a girl who could drive. She wasn't just a pretty face with a need for thrills. She was the daughter of the man who was trying to put my family out of business.

Marco slapped a hand on my shoulder, chuckling. "Hot damn! She's a Montclair."

I didn't respond.

Marco laughed. "That's like crashing full-speed into a wall."

Perhaps it was.

Perhaps I should have slammed on the brakes.

I grinned sarcastically. "Good thing I enjoy speed."

But as I gazed at the screen, seeing Jules standing beside the man who could destroy my world, I knew one thing for sure.

She was off-limits.

Then, as if the universe had a sense of humor and wanted to show me how royally screwed I was, the garage door groaned open.

And there she was, standing there right in front of me.

Jules.

Standing in my garage like it was home. Gazing dead at me, chin held high, hands stuffed into the pockets of her pink designer suit, looking at me as if last night hadn't shifted anything.

"Need a tune-up," she said, her voice smooth, unreadable.

Everything shifted at that moment.

And I knew I was in so much trouble.

XoXoXo

CHAPTER 5: RIVALS IN THE GARAGE

Juliet "Jules" Montclair

I returned the antique stopwatch to its velvet pouch, positioning it exactly where it had been. The Montclair showroom remained dark, the security system none the wiser that it had ever been breached. Because I had been the one to murder it from the outside. Romy believed he'd broke in, believed he'd danced with danger and won, but the reality was—I'd had his hand in mine the whole time, out of sight.

And that kiss. That crazy, bold, impossible kiss on

the roof.

I hadn't told anyone that it was my first kiss. Wouldn't ever tell him. Not when I'd spent years perfecting the art of appearing untouchable, unimpressed. And yet, I could still feel the heat of his mouth against mine, the way he tasted like smoke and adrenaline. The way, for one suspended second, it had felt like I belonged to something that wasn't a name or a legacy, but just a moment—just him.

But at school, it was as different as day and night.

"Street racers are nothing but lowlifes with death wishes," Sara Lin scoffed, clicking a manicured nail against her phone. "Seriously, if they want to wreck their cars and their lives, who are we to prevent them?"

Sara was effortless. She knew precisely what to say, precisely when to laugh, precisely how to fold herself into whatever space would make her shine the brightest. She wasn't merely my best friend—she was my blueprint. The girl I was meant to be.

Daughter of a tycoon of luxury real estate, Sara knew the game of fitting in. She recognized which frocks generated headlines, which rumors were potent, which transgressions might be forgotten if you smiled.

She navigated our world as if she'd been born carrying a map, and if ever I strayed off track, she was there to bring me back.

The other girls giggled, flipping their hair, their designer purses clinking gently as they adjusted. They had no idea. No idea what it was like to be behind the wheel, to slice through the darkness with only speed and ability between you and the void.

"They probably think they're rebels or something," Leo Mercier chimed in, rolling his eyes. "Like, congrats, you made it three blocks before you got busted."

Leo Mercier was the type of guy who strode into a room and commanded it to shift itself to accommodate him. And, all right, it usually did. Son of Laurent Mercier—the man who could probably afford to purchase half of Toronto if he so chose—Leo had grown up on power, honed to a shine. His shoes never scuffed, his tie never became untidy, and his smirk was always perfectly calibrated to be a mixture of arrogance and charm.

We'd grown up together. Playdates planned like corporate mergers, coordinating outfits for boat parties, a thousand pictures of the two of us standing a little too close together—evidence of an implicit agreement. The Mercier and Montclair dynasties were exploring the concept of a merger, and how better to seal that than with their offspring?

Leo never told me so, but I saw it in the way that he looked at me at those revolving-door galas, in the way that his hand touched my wrist just a heartbeat too long. He liked me. Or perhaps he liked the potential of me—the way our surnames sounded together, the way we photographed in the high-gloss pages of Society Toronto.

But the thing with Leo? He only liked stuff he could possess.

I stifled a bored smile, resisting the temptation to tell them just how mistaken they were.

"Perhaps they simply enjoy the high," I said airily, probing.

Sara snorted. "Or perhaps they are merely desperate. Consider it—boys like that? No future. No funds. No influence. Just losers grasping at a stupid high before they burn out."

Her words twisted in me, more than they ought to

have. Because she was mistaken about the money and the power. Romy had neither, but I'd never seen anyone burn so hot.

"Would you ever?" Leo asked without warning, eyes flicking to me with the laziness of someone who'd never had to risk anything. "Race?"

I caught Sara's eyes flicking to me. Because she loved Leo too. Not that she'd ever confess it. Not to him. Not to me.

Instead, she did her job—flawless, impenetrable, best friend, right hand. Always there, always in his circle. And if it would have killed her to see the way he looked at me, she never gave it away.

Sara Lin did not lose. Not in this life.

And that's why I never told her I was playing another game. One she didn't even know existed. One that reeked of gasoline and sounded like the rumble of a car engine at midnight.

I smiled, slow and deliberate. "Please. I have better things to do."

And so it went, the talk, with Leo satisfied, Sara reclining into her familiar complacent confidence that I would ever be one of "them". That I was meant to be in marble halls and choreographed destinies, not behind the wheel, slicing through the shadows.

But I didn't remain there for the remainder of the day. I left class, walked into my car, and headed directly home. Directly to the garage.

The smell of metal and gasoline hung heavy in the air as I entered, heels clicking on the smooth concrete before I removed them and replaced them with a pair of worn sneakers I'd left under the workbench. The Montclair house was immaculate, polished to within an inch of its life, but the garage? The garage was all mine.

Cutting class had become second nature, sneaking out of school property and into the garage as if I was moving between two worlds. It was easier to breathe there, under the hood of my car, where the world was a place of horsepower and precision tuning rather than expectations and slick deception.

But I wasn't as invisible as I believed.

Someone was watching. I just hadn't caught on yet.

The '67 Mustang rested in the middle, hood up, anticipating. My father had declared it a vanity project—a trophy to show, not to use. He hadn't a clue what I had done to it. What I'd transformed it into.

I passed a hand over the frame, the chill of metal bringing me back to earth. This was real. The burden of expectation, the prison of my last name—they didn't apply here. Not in the whine of a ratchet, not in the purr of an engine that I had taken apart and put back together myself.

The engine was taken apart to its core, grease coating my hands as I labored. It was simpler this way—no expectations, no crushing burden of being Juliet Montclair, no galas or obligatory smiles. Just me, the machine, and the only thing that had ever truly been mine.

By dinner time, I was back in my Montclair uniform—shined, poised, pretending. Dinner was all sharp silverware and tension, my father hardly glancing up from his phone as he ranted about the irresponsible degenerates making the city a playground for crime.

"These street racers," he grumbled, putting down his knife. "They think they own the city. They think the rules don't apply to them."

I maintained a blank face, cutting into my steak.

He didn't register that I hadn't touched it. I was

too busy keeping my face expressionless. Too busy not thinking of Romy.

"Tomorrow," he went on, "there is a press conference. You will attend." His gaze finally met mine, unyielding and calculating. "Presentable, looking.""

I choked back the urge to protest. As if it would make a difference. Victor Montclair did not ask—he commanded.

My father ruled his world with an even hand and a more vicious tongue, and when at last he shoved back from the table, he did not even give me a glance. "Be ready at noon." Then he was out of sight, his footsteps dying into the wide, deserted hallways of the house.

The instant he vanished, I let go of breath.

And that's when I did not see Nia come in, but felt her there before she spoke.

"You're playing a dangerous game, chérie."

Her tone was gentle, but there was something in it—something sharp, something knowing. I looked up. She was standing by the table, arms folded, eyes fixed on mine like she could see right through me.

I laughed, leaning back in my chair. "I have no idea

what you're talking about."

She didn't blink. She didn't smile. She walked closer, reaching down to curl her fingers around my wrist, catching me before I could even think about stepping back. Her hand was warm, firm, as she reversed my palm to expose the telltale thin smudges of grease remaining on my skin.

A dead giveaway.

Her grip tightened just slightly. Not enough to hurt. Just enough to make a point. Then, slowly, she pulled a napkin from the table and began wiping my fingers clean.

"You think your father won't notice?" she murmured. "You think he won't see this life bleeding into his?"

I swallowed.

"I'll handle it," I said.

Nia exhaled slowly, folding the napkin in half before putting it aside. "I hope so." Her tone softened, but her gaze remained keen. "Because if you don't, ma fille, it will handle you."

The baby pink suit was a joke, but a good one. A precisely calculated maneuver. The picture-perfect

Montclair heir—soft, poised, compliant. The good daughter. No one would ever suspect what lay beneath.

I smoothed my blazer, the silk lining against my skin, and folded into my seat next to my father. He hardly noticed me. No shock there. His whole attention was on the stage, on the cameras, on the immaculate image he'd spent his life building.

The mayor stepped up to the podium, flashing his signature politician's grin. "And now, my good friend, Victor Montclair, has some thrilling project to share."

I already suspected it would be terrible. I wasn't ready for how terrible.

My dad moved forward, buttoning his navy suit jacket with such ease. "In order to crack down on illegal street crime and risky auto enterprises," he announced smoothly, "we are undertaking a city-wide initiative to close down all unlicensed, criminal auto shops."

The blood dropped from my face.

Cruzer Auto & Body.

Romy's family. His world.

I braced myself to remain motionless, to maintain a neutral face, even as my gut contorted itself into knots. My father's words droned on—community safety, city alliances, the need to close down these so-called criminal operations. I didn't hear any of it. My fists balled in my lap, nails pressed into my palms.

This wasn't an attack on crime. This was personal. This was a war declaration.

I should have known. My father never made a move without counting his victories. And now he was taking on the underground culture, after individuals such as Romy, after the mechanics who toiled under humming fluorescent lights, after the drivers who lived for the thrill of speed.

The people who, to him, would never be quite good enough to walk on the same streets as men such as himself.

The audience applause jerked me out of it. My dad spun around, hoping I would grin, would pretend.

So I did.

I grinned at the cameras. I allowed them to take their immaculate photos. And then, once it was done, I walked away.

The urge to go over there was instinct.

I didn't think. I just acted, pushing my way out of

the press conference, sliding into my car, holding the wheel so hard my knuckles hurt. The city whizzed by— gray skyscrapers, neon lights, the flash of streetlights on my windshield. I didn't slow down.

I couldn't.

I came into the lot too hard, tires throwing up clouds of dust as I braked. The garage was a blur of activity—sparks streaming from welding torches, heavy bass music shaking through the air, the smell of oil and sweat and something unmistakably Romy.

As soon as I entered the garage, I sensed the change in the air. The warmth of it, the tension that was not spoken. And then I saw him.

He was slumped against a car, arms folded, dark eyes unyielding. Romeo Cruzer—regarding me as if I were something he regretted having ever touched.

I despised it. The way he could make my stomach turn by mere presence.

He didn't say a word as I moved in closer. Just let his eyes run over me, noting the stark contrast between my neatly pressed suit and the grease-splattered concrete my heels rested upon.

"Didn't expect to see you again, Montclair," he

said, voice tight, icy.

"I didn't know," I said, bypassing small talk. "About my father. About the crackdown."

Romy released a harsh, mirthless laugh. "Sure. Because rich girls always know what Daddy's doing."

I paused. "I didn't know about any of it. I swear."

He cleaned his hands on a rag, finally looking at me. His face was expressionless, but his eyes—they blazed.

"You expect me to believe that? That you— princess of Toronto, with your perfect life—had no idea your daddy was coming for my family?"

The words hit harder than they should have. "It's not perfect."

He scoffed. "Yeah, real tragic. What, your latte was the wrong temperature? Your Wi-Fi went out?"

"You don't know anything about my life, Romy."

"And you don't know shit about mine." I bristled. "You think I wanted this to happen?"

"I think it doesn't matter," he replied calmly. "Because it's happening, whether you want it to or not."

My throat constricted. "Romy—"

"Save it, Montclair."

There it was again. Montclair. Not Jules. Not even Juliet. Just my last name, spat out like an insult.

I breathed, trying to quell the frustration simmering beneath my skin. "I came here because I wanted to talk."

"Well, I don't." He shoved off the car and turned away. "Go home, princess."

The silence hung, heavy with something unsaid. Something in me broke. Something dangerous.

Then I smiled, slow and deadly. "Race me."

He froze. Slowly turned back around. His face unreadable. "What?"

"Race me." I straightened my shoulders. "If I win, you fix my car. If you win, I leave you alone."

The garage fell silent. The kind of silent that indicated people were listening. Watching.

A slow, sharp grin spread over Romy's face. "You want to lose that much?"

I raised a brow. "That sure of yourself?"

He hadn't replied before another voice intervened. "I like this."

I spun around.

A man I didn't know walked towards us, all loose confidence and cocky humor. Dark curls, sharp jaw, the sort of presence that caused people to move without even knowing they were giving him space. Grease-stained hands and a chain around his neck, the flash of a Saint Christopher pendant in the fluorescent light.

"Must be the notorious Montclair," he told me, eyeing me up and down like I was some shiny new model on the assembly line. "Didn't expect to see you in this way."

I raised an eyebrow. "And you are?"

He smiled. "Marco Cruzer. The cousin."

Marco Cruzer. Romy's cousin. The unofficial grandmaster of every street race worth watching.

He, let out a low whistle. "Shit, just got interesting. Alright, I'm in charge."

Romy eyed me like he was deciding whether or not to call my bluff. "You're serious?"

I grinned. "What's wrong? Scared of losing to a Montclair?"

That did it.

He clapped a hand on Romy's shoulder. "Come

on, primo. What's the harm?"

Romy exhaled through his nose, annoyed. "The harm is that she's not ready for this."

Marco tilted his head, considering me. "Oh, I think she is," he said, winking. "And I wanna see it."

Romy held my gaze. There was something dangerous there. A warning.

"You really want this?" he asked.

I nodded. "More than anything."

His jaw flexed. Then, finally, he said, "Fine. Let's race."

Relief flooded through me, but it was short-lived.

Romy nodded toward my car—my everyday car, the one I'd pulled up in, not some souped-up machine built for speed. "But you race in that."

I frowned. "What?"

"That's the deal. You race in the car you came in." His voice was calm, even. But I wasn't stupid. I knew exactly what he was doing.

My stomach tightened. My car wasn't built for this. It was quick, sure, but not Mustang-quick. Not custom-tuned, stripped-for-speed quick.

I could back out. Call it unfair.

But then I saw it—the flicker in Romy's eyes, like he was waiting for me to fold. Like he wanted me to.

I clenched my jaw. "Fine," I said, lifting my chin. "I don't need an advantage to beat you."

Marco let out a low whistle. "Damn. Now I really wanna see this."

The track was an open stretch of asphalt, slick with the threat of rain. No roaring crowds, no flashing headlights, no whispered bets. Just us—three figures under a dark sky, the hum of engines filling the silence.

Marco stood between our cars, arms raised.

Romy was in his Mustang, sleek and deadly. And me? I was in my daily driver. My car wasn't built for this. But that didn't mean I wouldn't try.

The engines roared.

Marco's hands dropped.

We launched forward.

The engines growled.

Marco's hands fell.

We shot forward.

The world went blurry, speed crashing into my chest like a second pulse. Each shift, each second mattered. Romy was in front—barely. I strained harder, the engine protesting, the tires digging into the road like claws.

Romy was fast—faster than I'd expected but I pushed harder. Not because I wanted him to work on my car.

Because I needed him to see me.

It was close.

Too close.

The finish line was in front of me. I could sense Romy alongside me, could sense his presence like a second shadow.

And then—I came in first.

I crossed the finish line half a second before he did.

Barely. By inches.

But barely still meant I won.

I stepped out of my car, panting, triumphant. Romy was already standing outside, hands on hips, shaking his head.

"I won," I announced, grinning.

He let out a quick breath. "Yeah. You did."

Tension flared between us, like lightning on a summer night. I took a step in, speaking quietly just for him. "Looks like you're fixing my car, Cruzer."

His jaw clenched. "Looks like it."

I should have left. But I didn't.

And neither did he.

A slow smile curled at my lips.

My father wanted me to be untouchable. He wanted me to be predictable. But Romy? He was a wildfire I was starting to think I might let consume me.

And for the first time in my life, I was willing to burn.

xoxoxo

CHAPTER 6: BREAKING ALL THE RULES

Romeo "Romy" Cruzer

The raid struck in the morning.

The battering ram to the front door, red-and-blue strobes cutting through morning fog. I was wakened by the shouting, the thumping heavy boots, and the nauseous crack of wood shattering.

And then—chaos.

Cruzer Auto & Body wasn't a garage; it was the pulse of my family. It was where my dad made a name for himself, where my uncle Rafa balanced the books, where I spent half my life with grime under my fingernails and an engine rumbling beneath my hands. And now—

Now, it was swarming with police.

"Toronto PD! Put your hands where we can see 'em!"

Police descended upon the shop like locusts, sweeping through the bays, overturning toolboxes, toppling shelves. Dad was already out there, shouting, his voice low and mean. Uncle Rafa stood next to him, arms folded over his chest, as Detective Harris—his badge shining under the garage fluorescents—strode through the destruction like he owned us.

I knew Harris. We all did. He'd been after us for years, trying to connect Cruzer Auto & Body with the chop shops, the street races, the lost luxury cars that vanished off showroom lots like specters at midnight.

He believed we were staging more than races— believed we were part of the same stolen-car loop he'd been working on taking down for months.

And perhaps he wasn't mistaken.

I slipped out the back before someone saw me. Didn't travel far.

"Don't move, Cruzer."

Harris jerked me back, pushing me against the hood of a tow truck. My heart throbbed in my ears.

"Morning, Detective," I mumbled, fighting down the urge to throw a punch. "A little too early for a call, don't you agree?"

His lips curled. "We received an anonymous tip that some hot cars passed through this garage. Stolen parts, perhaps. You wouldn't happen to know anything about that, would you?"

I didn't flinch. "Nah. Just a family operation here."

"Right." Harris' gaze covered the shop. Officers ransacked toolboxes, examining VINs, taking apart dashboards. One tipped over a metal shelf, sending parts cascading everywhere. My dad was yelling, my mom begging.

"Hands where we can see them," a uniform growled, pushing Marco into the workbench. My cousin gave me a look over his shoulder, half enraged, half resigned.

"Detective." My dad's tone was icy. "This is harassment."

Harris didn't flinch. "This is an investigation." He

turned, eyes focusing on me. "And I think your boy here may be able to tell us something."

I didn't budge. Didn't blink.

They never had anything. They always didn't have anything.

But that didn't discourage them from showing up.

And this time, it wasn't just the garage. It was her.

Uncle Rafa's fingers wrapped around my arm, his grip bruising. "This is the Montclairs' fault," he growled. "That girl is trouble, Romy. You keep your mouth closed and your back to her."

I pulled away.

"You don't know that."

"Don't I?" Rafa's glare could slice steel. "You think it's a coincidence? You let some rich girl into your world, and now the cops are at our door? Open your damn eyes, Romy. She's poison."

I wanted to fight. To tell him he was crazy.

But I didn't.

I didn't need to.

Because on the other side of the garage, Marco caught my gaze. And in the split second before he broke it, I saw it—the guilt.

He'd said so.

But I couldn't help but think of her.

Didn't matter I repeated the instruction of letting it go. Didn't matter that the garage was raided, Uncle Rafa breathing down my neck, Jules and I having to coexist in different worlds.

None of those things mattered.

Because I knew what I'd seen.

No way in hell that car of hers had bested mine.

I'd let her win.

And I didn't even know why.

Perhaps it was the look she had in the back of the car, the brief instant when our eyes locked before she shot past the finish line—wild, crazy, alive in a manner that left me with an aching chest.

Perhaps it was that nothing—nothing at all—that had encouraged me to lose.

Or perhaps it was simply Jules.

Whatever it was, it tormented me.

I was back in the garage that evening, hands deep in grease, tinkering with my Mustang as if repairing a perfect car could repair the chaos in my mind. Marco was stretched out on a worn-out couch in the corner, scrolling through his phone, observing me as if he could read my mind.

"Still pining for her?" he asked, far too entertained.

I didn't glance up. "Shut up."

"Man, you let her win." He whistled low. "That's some real Romeo and Juliet shit."

I slammed the hood shut. "I don't lose."

Marco snorted. "Except when she's behind the wheel."

I gave him a look, but he wasn't lying.

Because for the first time in my life, I wasn't sure if I was interested in a rematch.

Or if I just wanted her.

I knew that wasn't supposed to be anywhere near the Montclairs.

They owned half the goddamn city, and if anyone caught me sliding into their existence, I wouldn't leave in one piece.

But Jules was different.

She wasn't marble floors and wine tastings and six-figure sports cars sitting idle in a climate-controlled showroom.

She was this—fingers in the grease, bruised knuckles from gripping bolts, sleeves rolled up as she wiped oil onto the leg of her jeans, completely unphased by it.

I emerged from the shadows, moving slowly. "Didn't know heiresses worked with their hands."

Jules leapt, turning, a wrench gripped tightly in her hand like a weapon. When she spotted me, she let out a sigh. "What the hell, Romy?"

"Relax, princesa. You left your secret door open."

Her lips compressed, unmoved. "And your immediate thought was breaking and entering into my garage?"

"More like immediate thought was seeing what you were hiding." I took a look around, my eyes scanning the line of cars. Most were oldies— restoration projects in different stages of undress—but one stood out.

The one she'd beaten me with.

I smiled. "So you want to explain to me how in the world this little engine was able to keep pace with my Mustang?"

Jules paused, and then dropped the wrench with a

clatter. "I had tuned the engine myself."

I arched a brow. "Bullshit."

She folded her arms. "You really believe I don't know how to work on an engine?

I met her gaze. The only problem was, I did believe her. Which was perhaps more perilous than anything else.

My hand touched the hood of her vehicle. "You got tools?"

Her eyes creased in concern. "Why?"

I grinned. "Because you raced me with a goddamn commuter car, baby. Let's make it worth the streets."

For an hour, we labored. Together. Hands in the grease, elbows bumping, the smell of motor oil heavy in the air. And for an instant—for a breath—there was no Montclair and Cruzer. No bloodlines, no warnings, no rules.

Only two individuals who understood what it was to love the open road.

Jules leaned back, swiping her wrist over her cheek, leaving grease streaked along her jaw. "You know," she said softly now, "this is the only thing that makes me feel—" She broke off. Breathed. "Free."

I got that.

Too well.

I braced against the car, observing her. "We don't have to be what they say we are, Jules."

She glared at me then, something primal flashing in her eyes. But before she could respond, her phone beeped. She stared at the screen and flinched.

"Shit." She scooped up her bag. "I have to leave. Sara's party is tonight, and I said I'd be there."

I grinned. "Damn, and I thought I was going to be your plus one."

Jules laughed, but I saw the flash of something else. Amusement. Perhaps desire.

I moved in closer. "Lucky for you, I'm busy tonight."

"Yeah?" She leaned her head to one side, playing with me. "What's so important?"

I smiled.

Stealing a car.

Sara Lin's end-of-school masquerade every year was a who's who of the wealthy and irresponsible. A mansion bash, expansive pools and neon lights, champagne pouring like water. The type of place I had no right to be.

But I wasn't here to party.

I was here for a car.

Leo Mercier's Bugatti parked in the gated driveway, a custom job that cost more than my dad's entire garage. The idea was easy—jump in, grab the keys, and jump out.

What I hadn't anticipated was her.

Jules on the dance floor, lost to the music, lost to the moment. Her dress clung to her like sin, dark blue silk billowing against her legs as she danced. I wasn't meant to stop.

I wasn't supposed to want.

But then she turned, and my breath was caught in my throat.

Because she was dancing with me.

I didn't even think—I stepped in, hands grasping her waist, yanking her against me. She gasped, but didn't move away.

"Thought you were busy," she whispered.

I grinned, fingers curling into the material at her hip. "Changed my mind."

Her hands crept up my chest. "Dangerous game

you're playing, Cruzer."

I leaned in close, my lips against the rim of her ear. "I don't play fair, princesa."

The song changed. The crowd disintegrated. My fingers brushed the base of her neck, her breath on my jaw.

Then—havoc.

"JULIET!"

Tyson Vega.

Shit.

I hadn't even had time to turn around before he charged, plowing through the dancers like a bull with red fury.

Jules seized my wrist. "Run."

I hesitated for half a second—too long.

Tyson was close on us, face contorted with anger.

Jules didn't hesitate. She pulled me hard, and then we were moving—bumping through bodies, shooting through the throbbing neon mist of the party.

Someone yelled. Another voice helped. The crowd was realizing what was happening.

Tyson was closing in.

My heart throbbed. I clamped my hand around

Jules', fought through the melee, past the open bar, past the dazed looks and spilling drinks.

A side door—half ajar, faint light streaming through.

I drew her out of it.

One final look back over my shoulder—Tyson was within a stride or two, anger blazing in his eyes, fists tight.

We sprinted out into the darkness, gasping, giggling, racing.

Hand in hand.

xoxoxo

CHAPTER 7: FAST HANDS

Juliet "Jules" Montclair

The night felt like adrenaline. Like something burning too hot, too quickly.

We sprinted, winded and gasping, into the road, my heartbeat slamming against my chest. The party raged on behind us—glinting bodies, flashing lights, a cloud of privilege hanging heavy in the air. But for Romy and me, all of it no longer mattered. Only the beat of our feet on concrete and the buzz of electricity between us.

Then I saw the car.

Oh, you've got to be kidding me.

Tyson Vega's Ferrari parked out front like a golden invitation. Sleek, black as sin, and, more significantly, open. I stepped back to Romy, still heaving in the chest area, and already knew what that sparkle in his eye was telling me.

"No." I shook my head, taking a step back. "Absolutely not."

His smirk was slow, cocky. Enraging. "Relax, princess. He won't even know it was me."

"Not the point! That's my cousin's vehicle—"

"Better and better."

I didn't have time to stop him, he slipped into the driver's seat, opened the dash, and—God have mercy—hotwired the son of a gun like it was second nature. The engine hummed to life, smooth and deadly. He glanced up at me, one hand on the wheel, the other drumming the seat next to him.

"Get in, Jules."

Every rational thought yelled at me to get out. To be the girl I was taught to be, to be concerned with repercussions, to recall the gravity of my last name. But something about Romy Cruzer had rebellion feeling like liberty.

I got in.

As soon as the tires screamed on the pavement, I felt it—live, crazy, irrefutable. We sped down Toronto's night-lit streets, wind rushing through the rolled-down windows, the sound of the city fading into the background. Romy drove like he breathed—quick, sure, never in control.

I should have been angry. I should have been terrified. But all I was, was alive.

I looked over at him, seeing the way his fingers curled around the wheel, the set of his jaw in concentration. The streetlights cast him in glints of gold and shadow, a boy never owned by anyone, and yet somehow, tonight, he was owned here. With me.

"This is a terrible idea," I grumbled.

Romy grinned, turning to me with that wicked smile. "And yet, you're still here."

I despised the fact that he was correct.

I despised more that I didn't mind.

But our argument began when he drove into a vacant lot, the Ferrari rumbling like a beast in the darkness. Romy had driven us into a vacant lot—silent, dark, the sort of place things were lost. People vanished.

I pushed the door open, stepping into the cool bite of the night. "You find this amusing?"

Romy tagged behind at his own speed, propped against the car as if he didn't have a care in the world. As if he hadn't just upended my whole life off its nicely constructed rails. "I find it amusing. Come on, Montclair, admit it, you didn't hate it at all."

"Not the point!" My words escaped, lost in the vacant lot. "You took my cousin's car. Do you have any idea what a mess you just pulled me into?"

His smirk wavered, just barely. "You got in, Jules. Nobody made you."

I gasped in air. Hell, he was right—I had gotten in. I had allowed myself to feel the high, allow myself to taste a world that wasn't mine to have. And that frightened me more than anything.

I stepped back, running my fingers through my hair, attempting to find the words to say something—anything—without sounding a complete hypocrite.

And then suddenly—fire.

Romy was behind me, close enough that the

warmth of his breath grazed my bare shoulder. I didn't move. Didn't breathe.

"Why do you do it?" I whispered.

His voice was low, rough. "Do what?"

"This." I gestured at the car, at the night pressing in around us, at the raw, electric charge between us that I couldn't shake. "The racing, the stealing, the constant need to run."

He didn't respond at first. When he did, it was little more than a whisper.

"Because it's the only time I'm free."

The words struck deep, resonating somewhere below my rib cage. Because I understood that sensation. The crush of expectation, the chill, strangling hold of a future not my own. The way speed could strip that all away, even for a moment.

We weren't so different after all.

Something changed then—something more substantial than adrenaline, gentler than defiance.

I spun to confront him, and his eyes were already shadowed, regarding me as if he was committing each breath to memory. His hand rose, fingers just touching my jaw, as if he was allowing me the opportunity to prevent him.

I didn't.

I moved closer instead, closing the final inches between us, my fingers sliding under his jacket, past the chilly leather to the heat of his skin. His pulse beat beneath my fingers, rapid and wild.

Then his mouth was on mine.

And it was flame.

He followed the curve of my spine with his hands, fingers intertwining in my hair, angling my head just so to deepen the kiss. I dissolved into him, into the warmth, into the fit of his body against mine as if we were made for it.

My back bumped the Ferrari, the icy metal against my skin, a cold contrast to the heat of Romy's hands as they stroked down my waist. A little sound got past my throat—half sigh, half surrender.

God, this was crazy.

Because this wasn't merely a kiss. This was crashing at top speed. This was losing control and enjoying it.

Romy's lips traced a slow, agonizing path down my jaw, my pulse stuttering at the scrape of stubble against my skin. His hands burned through my dress, gripping my hips, holding me in place.

Then—just as fast as he started—he pulled back.

I blinked, breathless, my fingers still tangled in his jacket. "What—"

He exhaled, a low, rough sound, pressing his forehead to mine. "I'm on a schedule, Jules."

I gazed at him, bewildered. "What?"

A slow smile creased his lips, but his voice was gruff, unsteady. "If we don't end this now, I'm not ending it at all."

The space between us grew heavy with unspoken words, the tension we'd left between our mouths.

I swallowed, my heart still racing in my chest. "So what now?"

Romy took a step back, running his hand through his hair as if he needed room to breathe. "I lose the car. Then I take you up in mine."

I took a moment to wrap my head around it. Then—

I laughed.

Because this was crazy. Because he was crazy. Because I had no business saying yes, and yet I already knew I would.

Romy abandoned the Ferrari somewhere he didn't mention to me, saying Tyson would "find" it sooner or later. Then he came to get me in his own car, and we drove.

No where, no idea—just us and the city laid out before us.

Like a dream, sliding between the veins of Toronto—through alleys buzzing with neon, over waterfronts colored in silver and blue. We grabbed greasy takeout from a 24-hour diner, eating it on the hood of his car like we had all the time in the world. He made fun of the way I struggled with the chopsticks, I called him out on how he inhaled his food like he hadn't eaten in days. We argued over music, over favorite cars, over whether or not he'd actually let me drive his. (He wouldn't. Coward.)

For the first time in eternity, I felt weightless.

But all good things must end sometime.

The city whizzed by in stripes of light and darkness, but the closer we came to my neighborhood, the denser the night got. I edged in my seat, the buzz of the hot-wiring a car already wearing off, replaced by something harder, icier.

"Let me out at the corner," I said, my voice tight.

Romy didn't even flinch. "Not going to happen."

I let out a sharp breath. "Romy, listen to me. Just stop here—"

His grip on the wheel tightened. "I'm not scared of them."

My throat closed. Of course he wasn't. That was exactly the problem.

"It's not about being scared," I said slowly. "It's about—"

"Letting them win?" he interrupted. "Not my style, Montclair.

The gates to the Montclair property towered in front of me, black and hostile. I felt the pressure of my surname bearing down on me, the certainty of what was to come next.

But Romy just drove on. Smoothly, steadily. Without apology.

And then I saw them.

A black sleek car sat in the driveway, headlights still illuminated, casting long shadows against the immaculate Montclair mansion. Two men stood just beyond the light—one loose, the other tight, curled like a snake about to strike.

Victor Montclair and Tyson Vega.

My father and my cousin.

As soon as the car came to a stop, I knew this was no accident. This was a reckoning.

And Romy?

He simply drew the keys from the ignition and grinned.

As if he'd been anticipating this entire night.

I hadn't even had a chance to release my hands from my lap before Tyson was marching towards me, teeth clenched, anger etched into each tight line of his body. His tailored blazer could only just hold back the anger brewing beneath.

"Where the hell is my Ferrari?"

Romy slowly breathed, as if this was some kind of inconvenience at worst. He rested against his door, relaxed, as if he hadn't just hotwired a $300,000 car and then taken me around the city joyriding. "You got evidence I stole it?"

Tyson's fists were bunched. "Don't play games with me, Cruzer."

The way he sneered the name—it wasn't an insult. It was a threat.

But before Tyson could attack, Victor raised a hand. And suddenly, the air changed.

This wasn't anger anymore. This was power—cold, absolute.

My father didn't have to yell to demand attention. He was a man who could have a person eliminated by telephone, who established his fortune through silence and authority. He advanced, faultless in his three-piece, every inch a king surveying his chessboard.

"Let him keep it," he said, as silky smooth as the best glass.

The words struck with a heavy impact, taking the air out of my lungs.

Tyson snapped his head toward him, incredulous. "What?"

Victor didn't look away from Romy. His gaze was sharp, assessing. Calculating.

"Consider it a gift."

The weight of the words made my stomach twist. A gift wasn't generosity. A gift meant something was owed.

Tyson let out a sharp laugh, disbelieving. "You're seriously going to let this low-life keep my Ferrari?"

"Your Ferrari?" my dad's voice was teasing. "The insurance was in my name." He looked at Romy once more, eyes black with something unreadable. "So yes, he can keep it. But..." His voice chilled, the air constricting like a noose. "Stay away from my daughter."

Silence.

It was long, jagged and choking.

I should've spoken up. I should've fought back.

But for the first time that night, I remained silent.

And Romy...

Romy only smiled. Slow. Threatening. The sort of smile that didn't back down. The sort that threatened this wasn't finished.

Not by a long shot.

xoxoxo

CHAPTER 8: FIRST CRASH

Romeo "Romy" Cruzer

The Ferrari was still warm.

Heat clung to the metal like a secret, the engine ticking softly in the silence of the garage. I leaned against the frame, arms crossed, watching my father run a hand over the hood. He wasn't looking at me. Just the car. His fingers traced the curves like he could read the story of its last ride, every rev, every sharp turn, every moment it belonged to me instead of Vega.

Marco let out a low whistle. "Tyson's gonna lose his damn mind."

He did.

The overhead fluorescents buzzed, casting long shadows over oil-stained concrete. This was where stolen cars got new names, where engines whispered secrets, where the Cruzer name meant something. Not respect. Not power. Just survival.

A few feet away, Tino Delgado was crouched by the driver's side, running diagnostics through a handheld scanner, his brows furrowed in concentration. The soft beeping filled the space between us. Tino had always been the one who knew how to defuse a situation before it exploded. He didn't have Marco's reckless streak or my father's iron will—his strength was quieter. Calmer. He was the kind of guy who'd put himself in front of a fight just to make sure no one walked away bleeding.

"It's clean. No tracker."

"Course it's clean," Uncle Rafa scoffed from across the garage, wiping grease from his hands with an old rag. "You think my nephew's dumb enough to bring a chipped ride home?"

Uncle Rafa was built like a pit bull—short, broad, all muscle and sharp edges. His knuckles were scarred, his mouth always set in something between a smirk and a threat. He was the kind of man who solved problems with his hands first and asked questions never. My father ran the business, but Uncle Rafa made things happen. He knew the city's black market like the back of his hand, knew how to make cars disappear like they never existed. He was a hothead, but he was brilliant. And dangerous.

I kept my expression neutral. I wasn't dumb. But I had been reckless.

My father, Raul Cruzer, exhaled through his nose—long, measured, deliberate. He pulled a cigar from his pocket, rolling it between his fingers before tucking it away. A habit. He hadn't smoked in years, but he still liked the weight of it. Maybe it reminded him of a time when we weren't one bad decision away from being permanently on someone's hit list.

"You know how this works, Romeo." His voice was calm. Too calm. "You bring them in, we strip them down. No souvenirs. No second thoughts."

I should've nodded. Should've given the same tired response I always did.

Instead, I said nothing.

Across from us, my mother, Gabriela "Gabi" Cruzer, stood in the doorway, arms crossed. Watching. Always watching.

Her voice was quieter than my father's, but it cut just as deep. "What did you promise her?"

Jules.

I met her eyes. "Nothing."

She exhaled, like she could already hear all the lies I hadn't spoken yet. "Then don't start now."

The silence stretched.

And then Marco, ever the peacemaker—or the chaos-stirrer, depending on the night—grinned, clapping a hand on my shoulder. "Alright, can we cool it with the family drama? I got an appointment with a bottle of whiskey and a girl who still thinks I drive an Audi."

My dad shot him a look, unimpressed. Marco just smirked and leaned against the workbench, his leather jacket creaking.

Tino, still crouched by the Ferrari, glanced up. "We doing this or what?"

My dad didn't answer right away. Just studied me, like he was waiting for me to do something—

anything—to prove I still belonged in this life. Then, finally, he nodded toward the car.

"Get to work."

Uncle Rafa grinned, grabbing a wrench. "Let's strip this bitch down."

And just like that, the moment was over.

This was how it always went. We didn't talk about what we stole. We didn't talk about what it meant. We just worked.

Because that was the rule.

Cars came in. We broke them down, wiped them clean, and sold them for parts—engines swapped, VINs burned, identities erased. If it was valuable, it disappeared. If it wasn't, it got scrapped. Every job had a price, and every price was paid in silence.

My father ran the business, but Uncle Rafa was the one who made things happen. He had a hot temper, a sharper tongue, and the kind of mind that could turn a scrap heap into a getaway vehicle in under an hour.

Marco handled distractions. If a deal needed a smooth talker, he was there. If a cop needed a reason to look the other way, he found one. If a job needed a getaway driver—well, he didn't just get us out. He made sure we were never seen in the first place.

Tino kept us grounded. He was the only one who still called me 'Romy' like it meant something, the only one who reminded me that we weren't just parts in a machine. He wasn't the best driver, wasn't the best at talking his way out of things, but when shit hit the fan, he was the one making sure no one bled out before they made it home.

And me?

I was the one who couldn't say no.

I picked up a wrench, jaw tight.

Because I could still hear Jules' voice in my head.

Because for the first time, I wasn't sure I wanted to do this anymore.

Meanwhile, Jules' father was tightening his grip, shoving her deeper into a world that had already written her future in gold-leafed contracts and champagne-stained promises. Dominic Langford. The name was everywhere. Their faces, side by side, frozen in photographs that told a story Jules never got to write.

He wasn't just some rich boy with a trust fund and a last name that opened doors. Dominic was legacy—

old money, auto empire, the kind of polished perfection that made men like Victor Montclair nod in approval. And the worst part? He actually loved her.

Not in the way I did, not in the way that burned. But in the way that hurt.

Maybe if things were different, if Jules wasn't a Montclair and I wasn't a Cruzer, if my name wasn't something her father spit like a curse—maybe she would've let herself love him back.

But love didn't matter when you were playing chess with men like Victor. Jules was a piece on the board, and Dominic was the king her father was positioning into checkmate.

Marco flicked his lighter, the flame catching the edge of his smirk. "You can't burn oil and water, hermano."

But I'd never been one to listen to warnings.

Jules showed up late that night. Or maybe I was just waiting too soon.

Her footsteps inside the garage barely made a sound, but I felt her before I saw her—an energy that didn't belong in a place like this. Too sharp. Too bright. Too much of something I knew I could never keep.

I stayed under the hood of the Camaro, letting the silence stretch. If I looked at her now, I wasn't sure I'd be able to stop.

"You lost?" I muttered, reaching for a wrench.

She didn't smile. "Just wanted to see you work."

My jaw tightened. "Dangerous game, Montclair."

She shrugged. "I'm used to those."

I let her stay. Maybe because I wanted her to see. Maybe because I wanted her to know the weight of this life, to feel the oil on her skin, the gasoline in her lungs. Or maybe because I was too damn selfish to turn her away.

For a while, she just watched. The steady hum of the city outside filled the spaces between us. When I finally looked up, she was tracing a finger along the edge of the workbench, a furrow between her brows like she was trying to memorize the shape of this world. Like she already knew she didn't belong in it.

"You ever think about leaving?" she asked, voice low.

I snorted. "Leaving what?"

"This. The cars, the streets. Your family." She hesitated, her eyes catching mine. "Me."

I exhaled sharply, wiping my hands on a rag. "Why would I leave something that makes sense?"

She looked down. "Because not everything that makes sense is good for you."

Something in her tone set my teeth on edge.

"What aren't you telling me?"

Jules hesitated. Then she reached into her bag and pulled out her phone, tapping the screen before holding it up. The glow of it lit her face in the dim garage, but my focus went straight to the image in front of me.

Jules. And Dominic Langford.

They stood side by side at some charity event, the kind with chandeliers and cameras and people who thought money meant power. She was wearing a dress that probably cost more than my father's garage. He had his arm around her waist. His grip was light, careful. Like he knew he was holding onto something breakable.

"My father's tightening his grip," she said quietly. "He wants the Montclairs and Langfords together. Business. Legacy. An empire built on cars and clean money." Her lip curled. "Well. Clean on paper."

I shoved the rag into my back pocket, shaking my head. "So what? He parades you around with some rich kid until you get sick of it?"

Jules didn't answer right away. She tucked her phone away like she didn't want to look at it either. "Dominic's not just some rich kid, Romy. He's..." She sighed, pressing her fingers to her temple. "He's good. He doesn't deserve this."

Something twisted in my chest, ugly and unwanted. "And what about you?"

Her smile was brittle. "I don't think that matters."

The words landed like a slap. My fists clenched. "Bullshit."

"It's not bullshit, it's my life!" Her voice cracked, and for the first time tonight, I saw something raw in her expression, something terrified. "You think I get a say in this? You think I can just—just walk away? From my father, from everything he's built?"

I stepped closer. "I think you want to."

She swallowed. Her breath hitched. "And if I did? What then? We run?" Her laugh was short, bitter. "You and me, in the wind like some bad movie? Romy, this isn't a fairytale."

"No. It's worse." Another step. "Because in fairytales, they don't fight for it. They just believe in fate and hope it all works out." I studied her, memorizing the way the moonlight turned her hair to silver, the way she still smelled like wind and recklessness. "You and me? We were never built for easy. But that doesn't mean we don't work."

Her breath shuddered against the night air. "We can never work."

"Why not?"

"Because my father would destroy you. Because Dominic—"

Another step.

"Because this world doesn't let girls like me love boys like you."

I was inches away now. Close enough to see every excuse flickering behind her eyes like she was reciting a script someone else had written.

"Because you deserve better," she whispered.

I tipped my head, hands flexing at my sides. "We both do."

Her breath hitched. And for one perfect, impossible second, she let herself believe in the fantasy.

Then I kissed her.

And for one perfect, impossible second, she kissed me back.

Marco's voice echoed in my skull, low and warning.

You can't burn oil and water, hermano.

I knew that. I'd always known that.

But maybe I wanted to watch it burn anyway.

×o×o×o

CHAPTER 9: TWO WORLDS COLLIDE

Juliet "Jules" Montclair

I hadn't anticipated the slap, but perhaps I should have. My father was never a man to waste words where violence would suffice.

Victor Montclair's anger was a quiet, smoldering thing, like an unbridled fire burning in the fireplace of our estate—held at bay only by the walls erected around it. His handprint didn't fade from my cheek, but his words did.

"You will never see that boy again."

The research reeked of stale bourbon and old leather, the air heavy with tension I had learned not to dare. My father walked the length of the room, the polished mahogany floors drinking in his every footstep. His steps were precise, calculated—just like the rest of him.

Ty stood in the doorway, arms crossed over his suit coat, eyes on me like I was some animal trapped in a cage. Perhaps I was.

"The Cruzers are criminals," my father continued, his voice like steel wrapped in silk. "And you—" he exhaled sharply, shaking his head as if I'd already disappointed him beyond repair, "—are a Montclair."

A Montclair. As if that was ever supposed to mean anything to me again. As if it was ever supposed to outweigh the way Romy looked at me like I was something greater than my last name, greater than the marble cage I'd grown up in.

Ty eventually pushed away from the doorway. "You have too much to lose, Juliet." His tone was gentler than my father's, but no less condescending. "You're soon to be engaged to Dominic. Do you really want to toss all that out for some street racer?"

Dominic Langford. The name hung in my chest, a weight I couldn't lose no matter how hard I tried. A man with soft hands and pricey cologne, the son of a successful auto investor family. Not cruel. Not unkind. But not Romy.

I gritted my teeth. "It's not your choice."

Ty snorted, chuckling under his breath, and shook his head as if I were a pouting child having a tantrum. "This isn't negotiable."

My dad turned to me then, his eyes cold and distant. "From this point forward, Tyson is with you. Always."

Ty gave me a sleepy grin, like this was a joke to him. "Think of me as your own personal shadow, cousin. I even vow to look the other way when you slip out. Once or twice."

I said nothing. What was the use? My father had made up his mind. My destiny was a business deal, a well-knit scheme that had been set in motion long before I knew anything about being a part of this family.

But I wasn't finished fighting.

Public dates with Dominic Langford were another

punishment.

He wasn't the bad guy in this fairy tale. The worst of it was that.

Dom was exactly the kind of man my father would approve of—wealthy, charming, a pedigree clean of scandal. And worst of all, he actually wanted me.

We sat at a table in some overpriced restaurant where the waiters spoke in hushed tones and the wine was older than we were. Paparazzi flashed their cameras from the street, their lenses capturing a love story that didn't exist.

Dom leaned across the table, fingers touching mine. He was feeling me out, testing the boundaries of how far I'd let him go before I'd push him away.

"You don't have to struggle so much," he told me, voice low, as if he was sharing a secret with me. "We could be good together."

I smiled for the cameras. "That's the difference between you and me. You still think I have a choice."

His jaw clenched, but he did not say another word. He loved me—at least, the version of me he believed he knew. The girl in the fitted dress, with a legacy etched in gold. Not the one who reeked of gasoline and asphalt.

Dom let out a breath, relaxing back, his fingers weaving through the condensation on his glass. "You think I have a choice?" he said at last. "You think I wanted this?"

That took me aback. "Didn't you?"

A bitter laugh. "Jules, I've loved you since we were children." He shook his head, something almost like remorse in his face. "Not that you ever noticed. You were always too busy running."

I forced myself to meet his eye. "And now?"

"Now you don't get to run."

His words lay between us, weighted with something I did not want to identify. Outside, the cameras continued to flash. Inside, the restaurant hummed around us, unaware of the war unfolding in the space between our bodies.

I allowed my gaze to fall to the linen tablecloth of white, seeing it as an altar. How would it feel? To relinquish, to accept this destiny, to permit Dominic to become my future and not my father's tool? A life with order, expectations I already comprehended. A marriage that worked, a spouse who would remain faithful, who would provide a gilded cage for me to reign from.

Children. Inheritors. A legacy to maintain.

For a moment, I indulged in the fantasy, allowed myself to dream what it would be like to be with a man who wasn't risky. Who wouldn't set me ablaze just for standing near him.

Then there was Romy.

I remembered him now, without thinking, the smell of motor oil and adrenaline pushing aside the choking tang of truffle risotto. I remembered the way he moved—reckless, sharp, as if he was perpetually a fraction of a second away from catastrophe. I remembered the way he gazed at me, as if he could penetrate every varnished deception, as if he knew the woman hidden behind the moniker and wanted her anyway.

Dominic wasn't a bad choice. But he wasn't Romy.

And that meant he was never going to be enough.

I raised my glass of water, masking my face as I slowly drank. Dom's eyes flashed to my mouth, but I looked away. The Langfords were scheming, just as my father had been. They coveted our wealth, our surname, our power. Perhaps if I were cunning, I'd play the game and let them believe they were winning.

But Romy's voice was in my mind, whispering of stolen nights and back-alley escapes, of the sort of love that was too hot to endure.

I put my glass down. "We should leave," I said.

Dom's mouth opened, but he did not dispute it. He simply nodded, ordered the check, and let the night devour what words he had been about to say.

I began keeping to myself in my garage, the sole property of this estate that felt mine. The mansion had a gazillion rooms—libraries, drawing rooms, reception areas—but this garage was the only area without expectations. Myself, my tools, and the hum of the cars that I shouldn't touch.

Romy caught up with me there.

He shouldn't have been there. I shouldn't have allowed him to come by. But when he leaned on the tool bench, gaze roaming over me like I was something that could be looked at, I knew I wasn't going to shove him out the door.

"Teach me," I replied.

His forehead creased. "Teach you what?"

"How to repair engines. The way that you do."

He raised his eyebrows. "You don't get your hands dirty, Montclair."

I took a step forward. "Perhaps I should."

He analyzed me, inclining his head to one side as if attempting to glimpse past the girl with the carefully groomed dresses and diamond-studded heritage. And then he sighed out his nostrils, shook his head like he already repented whatever it was that was going to come to pass.

"Fine," he grumbled, shoving away from the bench. "Come on."

I went along as he squatted beside the car's open hood that I had been pretending to repair, before he came along.

"This," he explained, thumping a knuckle on a metal cylinder, "is the alternator. If your car won't start and the battery is good, this is most likely the culprit."

I knelt down alongside him. "And how do you repair it?"

He gave me a dry glance. "You don't. You call me."

I rolled my eyes, pushing against his shoulder. He

didn't move.

"Chill out, Montclair. First lesson—identifying the pieces." He reached into the open engine, his fingers running over the belt looped around the engine. "Serpentine belt. Keeps everything going the way it's supposed to. Ever hear a squealing whine when you're driving?"

"Only when you talk."

Romy huffed a laugh, shaking his head before turning my wrist over and pressing my fingers against the rubber. His skin was rough, calloused from years of work, a stark contrast to mine.

"If it starts cracking or slipping, the whole thing can fail. You'd be stranded." His voice dipped lower. "Alone."

I swallowed. "And what, you'd come rescue me?"

His fingers stayed on mine for a beat too long. "If you called me."

Something in my chest knotted. I didn't reply. Couldn't.

Instead, I moved around him, nodding at a set of metal pipes. "What about that?"

"Fuel injectors," he breathed. "They regulate how

much gas reaches the engine."

I ran the tips of my fingers over them, then retreated, observing how grease smeared the skin. I should have been out of place here—this garage was not mine, not exactly. The tools, the scent of oil and rubber, the biting taste of gasoline in the air. It wasn't the world I was born into.

And yet, standing here, side by side with Romy, I had never felt more myself.

We continued working. He taught me to recognize parts by touch alone. He allowed me to struggle with bolts, his hands over mine when I messed up. We worked in silence initially, Romy's breath warm against my temple when he leaned in too close, my pulse stumbling over itself every time our fingers touched.

That evening, an unspoken agreement fueled between us. One that was constructed out of stolen time and pilfered moments, out of whispers shared between the rumble of an engine and the sound of a name that never should have been mine to call.

Romy. Romeo.

My phone vibrated. A text from Ty.

Family dinner. Langfords. Now.

I exhaled. "I have to go."

Romy nodded only. "Of course you do."

He paused, then continued, "If you ever need anything, call me. Whatever."

I didn't say a word. Just walked away. Because needing him was dangerous enough already.

Dinner was just as I knew it would be. Wine glasses clinked against one another, voices buzzed above plates of food I hardly touched, and then with an afterthought, Dominic's mother mentioned, "The engagement party will be in late August."

I put my fork down slowly, my heart pounding in my ears.

Dominic bristled. His gaze flicked to me, something indistinguishable there, something hesitant.

My father grinned, as if this was all a procedure. "A late summer wedding is a good idea. Keeps the media buzz steady."

Dominic's father nodded in approval. "Yes, and by winter, we can start making wedding plans. It's better to keep things moving."

Tyson reclined in his chair, taking his wine as if none of this was important. "Might as well get it over with, huh?"

Dominic gave him a hard stare. "It's not a business merger, Tyson."

"Oh, isn't it?" I cut through the stilted conversation.

Silence descended upon the table. My father's fingers drummed against the base of his glass, a warning without words. Dominic's mother tittered, as though I'd said something funny.

"Of course, we want you to be happy, Juliet," she said. "But this is more than about you, my dear."

And there it was. The truth, revealed in gentle words and a refined smile.

I could sense Dominic eyeing me, hoping I wouldn't cause a scene.

I didn't. I got up, placed a hand on my stomach, pretending to be sick. "Excuse me."

Then I slipped out, losing Ty long enough to reach the unused back gate of the Montclair estate.

Romy was already there.

I had texted him while I was at the dinner, one word.

Now.

He didn't question me when I got into the passenger seat, didn't require explanations. He simply turned on the car, the engine humming to life like it already knew how quickly we had to get out of there.

And as we sped away from the house, I allowed myself to breathe.

For a second. Nothing more.

The interior of his car smelled of him—of leather and gasoline, of something wild and alive. The windows misted from the contrast of the chilly night air and the heat pulsing between us, heavy enough to take my breath away.

Romy's hand was on the gear shift, fingers curling, as if he were attempting to remain steady. As if he weren't already on the precipice of something irrevocable.

I breathed hard, digging my fingers into the seats as he sped along, wild—the way I liked. The way he knew I craved.

We stopped somewhere hidden, a hidden corner of the city where the world wouldn't find us, wouldn't push its expectations against our skin like a burn.

"I don't want this life," I confessed, my words a

whisper. "I don't want to be a Montclair."

Romy looked at me in the faint light of the dashboard, his eyes gentler now, as if he could iron out the frayed edges of my disintegration with a glance. "Then don't be."

As if it were that simple.

I moved closer, bridging the gap between us. "Tell me your dreams."

He exhaled, one hand resting against my leg, hesitant. Testing. "You first."

So I explained. About the roads I wished to race, the cities I wished to visit, the weight I wished to shed from my throat. And then he explained his—the things he wished, the things he could not have. The things we both knew would never be ours.

And then I kissed him.

Not a tender kiss. Not the sort I learned to bestow at debutante dances, all prim restraint and exactness. This was ravenous, desperate—something pilfered in darkness, something that could never live in the light.

His fingers weaved through my hair, angling my head back, deepening the kiss so I was spinning. So I didn't care that we were mashed against the leather seats of his car rather than the silk sheets of a world that had already mapped out my future.

The windows had steamed up, obscuring the world beyond, but I hardly noticed. All I could see was how Romy was staring at me, as if I were something he could not touch, something he could not profane. And yet he touched me.

His lips caressed my jaw, tracing along the column of my throat, slow, almost worshipful, as if memorizing me just in case this was the final time. And perhaps it was.

A Montclair shouldn't have fallen for a boy like him. A girl like me shouldn't have been in the back seat of a car that reeked of speed and defiance, fingers struggling at buttons and zippers, dress sliding from my shoulders like it had never fit there in the first place.

His fingers followed the contours of my skin, setting something deep within my ribs alight, something that took my breath and with it, the world, which rocked on its axis. Not in fear, but in the way he regarded me. Like I was worth shattering the world.

There was no strategy. No grand gesture. Only us.

Fingers mapping skin, knotted arms, heat and

uncertainty. A silent form of desperation, the kind that led us to slow down even when everything else was yelling at us to speed up.

The gradual, paralyzing understanding that there was no turning back from this.

I didn't care.

For once in my life, I wasn't a Montclair. I wasn't an heiress with a script to follow, a daughter burdened by a name that never quite belonged to me. I wasn't a girl locked up in a realm of chill marble floors and mannered, toxic smiles.

I was a girl in the back of a car, loving a boy she wasn't supposed to.

And for a single night, that was enough.

But the world never allowed us to be enough.

The moment's rush dissipated, leaving only the weight of our breathing and the residual heat of skin on skin. Romy let out a breath, his arms constricting around me as I buried my face in the hollow of his shoulder, my fingers spreading over his pulse like I could commit it to memory, like I could seal it within me forever.

He kissed my hair, his lips against my temple

warm. "You okay?"

I nodded, still with my cheek against his chest. "You?"

A low, pleased sound. "Better than okay."

The afterglow encircled us, something warm, something unexpected. The leather of the back seat was cool against my exposed skin, but Romy was warm, unyielding.

I settled into him, my leg thrown over his, my arm draped across his belly.

I wasn't used to this. The silence. The peace.

"You know," Romy whispered after an extended moment of quiet, his fingers tracing lazy patterns down my spine, "we could just go. Drive until we reached the coast. Never glance back."

I grinned, although there was a constriction in my throat. "And do what? Live out of your truck?"

His chest vibrated with another soft laugh. "Could be worse."

I leaned my head, our eyes meeting in the soft light of the dashboard. "I think you'd tire of me."

"I think I wouldn't."

I swallowed hard. The words, the moment, the

feel of him sitting next to me—it was all too much. Or perhaps not enough.

I ran my fingers over the shape of his jaw, letting them rest against the rough line of stubble there. "If I ever need you—"

He grabbed my hand, intertwining his fingers with mine. "You call me." His tone was unyielding, leaving no doubt. "No matter what. No matter when."

I nodded, swallowing hard against the tightening in my chest. I wanted to think we could keep this—keep each other.

But some things weren't meant to last.

Romy's phone rang, the piercing sound cutting through the quiet.

I could sense him tense beneath me, sensed the moment crack before he'd even responded.

He reached for it, his jaw clenching when he looked at the caller ID.

Marco.

He flipped the call on, his tone low. "Yeah?"

Marco's voice sliced through the night. "You have to get in here. Uncle Rafa is looking for you."

Romy and I exchanged glances.

And our time was up, just like that.

xoxoxo

CHAPTER 10: A DEAL GONE WRONG

Romeo "Romy" Cruzer

My car still had her scent.

Like vanilla and something alive, something that had my hands trembling to this day as I clutched the wheel too hard. The memory of her touch still seared my skin, the pressure of her body against mine, her warm breath against my neck.

I'd never experienced anything remotely like that before. Not the sex, exactly, but her.

Jules Montclair, sharp tongue and sharper brain,

the girl who walked as if she was always running from something, as if she was designed to move at high speed but stuck in a cage of designer clothes and rehearsed smiles.

And for one night, she allowed herself to be wild. With me.

No titles. No names. No world on our shoulders trying to crush us. Only heat and hands, breathed whispers, and the way she breathed my name like it was something.

For the first time, I wasn't Romeo Cruzer, the boy driving hot wheels for a family that would never release him. I wasn't the boy who was trying to run away from his last name.

I was a boy in love with a girl he should never be with.

And then Marco called.

The moment I heard his voice, the post-Jules high came crashing down like a car into a wall.

"You have to get in here. Uncle Rafa is looking for you."

I didn't need to ask him why. If Rafa came seeking me, it wasn't because he wanted to dispense life lessons. It was because I owed him something.

And a Cruzer never turn their back on familia.

The shop tended to smell of oil and grease, but tonight it reeked of poor choices.

The kind that made you inhale them, thick and strangling, the kind that transformed lives. Shattered them.

Uncle Rafa sat in his favorite chair, legs splayed, fingers tapping against the armrest like a man with all the time in the world. He didn't. None of us did. But Uncle Rafa enjoyed pretending, and when Uncle Rafa pretended, the rest of us had to pretend too.

Marco was already there, slumped against the workbench, arms crossed. His hoodie was splattered with something dark—oil, perhaps, or blood. With him, either was possible. He was gazing at me, but his thoughts were somewhere I wasn't sure I cared to follow.

Rafa's gaze passed over me, resting on the new bruises on my collarbone. I could still sense Jules' fingers digging into my skin, her lips moving against mine, the pressure of her breath when she breathed my name like it was the only thing in the world.

Rafa smiled. "That Montclair girl keeping you busy?"

I didn't rise to the bait. "You called me in for a reason."

He leaned back, breathing like he was savoring this. Like seeing me squirm was the best part of his evening. "That's the beauty of rich girls, sobrino," he said, voice smooth, calculated. "They believe they're the ones playing the game, but they never anticipate the checkmate."

Marco snorted, shaking his head. "You're thinking too small, Rafa."

That got my attention. I shifted, looking between them. "What are you talking about?"

Marco stood up from the workbench, stretched his arms wide. "Montclairs. Their showroom. Their security." His tone became one of lazy assurance. "I have a contact, IT guy for one of their suppliers. Told me the system has vulnerabilities. Cameras? Rotating. Security? Burned out. Building like that, high-end cars coming in and out every day, you figure they keep an eye on all of them?"

I scowled. "You're trusting this on some guy's say-so?"

Marco gave me a look. "It's good intel, Romy."

"It's a risk," I retorted. "And as far as I know, risks killed people."

Rafa chuckled, dark and slow. "What's making you so anxious, sobrino? The job? Or the girl?"

I didn't answer. Because anything I said would be wrong.

He sat forward, eyes cold now. "I require her, Romy." His voice was steel with silk covering it. "I require her to trust you. To love you. For when the moment arrives, she's our in."

My hands curled into fists before I could catch them. "You want me to use her."

"I want you to see it through," Rafa corrected, his smile now gone, his voice cutting. "Her daddy's got more cash in that showroom than God himself. And with the right information? We go in, take what we need, and walk out clean."

The room seemed too cramped. Too close.

I shook my head. "It's not that easy."

Marco sighed. "You always do this, man. You hem and haw. You wonder. It's like you have no idea where you came from."

I glared at him, jaw clenched. "Something like that can get you six feet under."

Nothing. Even Rafa froze.

Marco's face set in a hard mask. "And yet here you are, in a garage that pays for your existence. Our existence. Your little affair with Montclair. You think you can have it both ways?"

Rafa snapped the tension with a low laugh. "He thinks he can be one of them."

I spun back to him, every muscle in my body tense and ready to snap. "And if I say no?"

He smiled. Slow. Cold. The kind that curled my stomach. "Then I remind you who you belong to."

There was no saying no.

Not to him. Not to this life.

And certainly not to the reality that, regardless of how much I might desire it, I could never actually have Jules Montclair.

Because one day, she was going to look at me and look exactly at what I was.

And that was going to be the day she walked away.

But the thing about Jules? She never did what I

anticipated.

I'd spent my life around people who wanted to prove themselves. Who had something to prove. But Jules?

She knew who she was. She was born into power, sculpted into something untouchable. But when she was with me, she wasn't untouchable at all.

She was fire.

And at the moment, she was leaning over the hood of a '73 Skyline, grease-covered hands, her hair tangled into a crumpled knot, looking at me as if she could see clear through the crap in my head.

"You're distracted," she said, cinching the bolt with a smooth turn.

I grinned. "Maybe I just enjoy watching you work."

She raised a flawless eyebrow. "You didn't bring me here to flirt. You brought me here because you're looking for something."

Damn. She did see through me.

I shrugged, wiping my hands on a rag. "Just considering security at Montclair Motors." I shot her a look. "You ever consider how I managed to get you that stopwatch?"

Jules smiled. "Did you really think I'd send you in blind?"

I froze.

She leaned forward, voice lowering to something softer, more sinister. "I disabled the security from the outside. A few codes and a remote access override was all it took." She tapped her temple. "Montclair brains, Cruzer instincts."

I let out a low chuckle, shaking my head. "So you wanted me to steal it."

She bit her lip. "I wanted to see if you could."

I ought to have felt relieved. But instead, I sensed something darker nestle in my ribs. Because I was going to take advantage of the girl who had already trusted me.

"I suppose I'll just have to keep testing you then," she whispered, playful, but there was something to her words. Something genuine.

She had no idea.

I manufactured a smirk, shoving my hands into the pockets of my jacket. "Careful, Jules. You keep making me do battles, and I might just start winning."

Her laughter was warm, playful. "Not tonight. Tonight, we win together."

The words cut at me like a blade.

Because tonight wasn't a race.

It was the race.

It was me and a masked up Jules, side by side against The Stray Dogs—the city's most vicious street racers. They didn't play by the rules, and they didn't like losing. They had a reputation for something more than speed. Anyone who crossed them ended up with a trashed car or worse, a broken face.

The second the flag fell, the world dissolved into neon lines and the electric thrum of the city at night. My fingers wrapped tight around the wheel, my foot jammed down on the pedal until I could feel the car respond under me, bucking forward with a snarl.

Jules sat beside me in the passenger seat, eyes scanning the road, voice tight and crisp over the din of the engine. "Left in three…two…NOW!"

I twisted the wheel tightly, tires shrieking as we just grazed the edge of the curb. The car from the Stray Dogs veered too close behind us, its headlights two angry eyes in the back of the rearview mirror. The driver wasn't following the rules—if there were any to follow. I saw a flash of movement as his partner leaned out the window and threw something.

Spike.

Jules noticed it at the same moment I did. "Shit— swerve right!"

I jerked the wheel, barely dodging the trap, but the other vehicle was already positioning itself next to us, its occupant grinning as if he had us where he wanted us. Then he swerved, hard, hoping to send us careening into a parked truck.

I gritted my teeth and let my instincts ride, feathering the brakes just enough to slide up behind him before pushing it again. Jules was still catching her breath before she yelled, "Ahead—narrow alley, forty meters. If we take it, they won't cut the corner."

I took a risk and glanced at her. "You sure?

She glanced over at me, firm and hot. "Trust me."

So I did.

I swerved left down the alley, the walls whizzing by in a flash of brick and paint. The Stray Dogs were half a second behind us. Half a second too slow.

A disgusting crunch sounded behind us as their

car crashed into the corner, metal folding up like tinfoil. I didn't brake until I was back on open road, my heart a war drum in my ears.

Then I heard it.

Crowds cheering.

The finish line was before us.

I barreled through it at top speed before allowing the car to slow, heart still racing. As soon as we skidded to a halt, Jules flung open the door and staggered out, panting and wide-eyed.

We had won—thanks to her—she tore off her mask, hair tumbling out, and turned to look at me, grinning.

"You let me win that day, didn't you?"

I could've lied.

But she had earned the truth.

I leaned in, voice low. "You'll be the only girl I ever let win me over."

She blinks. And then, just there, before the crowd, she kissed me.

I felt the moment click into place like a fragment of a puzzle I'd never known existed. And as the flashbulbs sparked, as the city watched, I realized something harsh and unavoidable.

I loved her.

And I was going to betray her.

By the time I returned to the garage, Jules' phone was already in my pocket. Felt heavier than it should—like guilt had a weight, like I could feel the betrayal against my ribs.

Marco leaned against the workbench, arms folded, looking at me like he already understood. He always understood.

"Took you long enough," he said, his voice edged with that particular impatience.

I handed him the phone. "Let's get this over with."

He one-handed it, turning it over in his hand, his face inscrutable. "You sure you want to do this?"

No.

I wished I could yank it back, tell him to forget about it, tell Rafa to stick this whole scheme up his butt. But that wasn't how this worked. There wasn't an out. There was only forward.

I made a forced smile. "What I want doesn't matter, does it?"

Marco looked at me, black eyes darting between

me and the phone, as if looking for something I wasn't in the mood to provide.

He let out a harsh breath and turned, moving toward Rafa's office. I trailed after him.

Within, Rafa was already sitting, reclining in his customary chair, his expression one of king on throne. His fingers tapped against the armrest lazily, his smirk slow and deliberate.

"About time," he told me. "Thought maybe you were having second thoughts."

I said nothing. There was no point. He could smell doubt as easily as he could smell blood in the water.

Marco pressed the phone into his hand. "Montclair's security is tight, but this? This gives us the inside track."

Rafa grasped it, turning it over with the same interest that a man like him only showed when there was money at stake. "So, what's the word?"

Marco rested against the desk. "Heard it from a trusted source—Montclair's security in their showrooms is lax. The kind you can drive a truck through if you hit it at the right moment."

I scowled. "Who's your source?"

Marco gave me a look. "You questioning me now?"

"I'm questioning anyone who believes attacking the Montclairs is a walk in the park."

Rafa chuckled, low and pleased. "Calm down, sobrino. If Marco vouches for the intel, it's solid."

I did not calm down. Not even remotely.

Because the thing is about life here? The instant you let your guard drop, you were as good as dead.

Rafa's smile sliced. "All we need then is timing. And as good fortune has it, your little girlfriend's phone holds the key."

My fists flexed. "She's not—"

He indicated with his hand. "Oh, don't bother me with the terminology. I couldn't care less what you refer to her. She's just a bargaining chip, and bargaining chips get victories.

Silence hung between us. My heartbeat thudded in my ears.

Rafa leaned forward, his voice silk on steel. "This robbery? It's going down. And now, courtesy of you, it's going down with an edge."

I swallowed hard, my mouth parched. I should've

been triumphant. Instead, something inside me churned.

Because I'd just given them the one thing that could kill her.

And once that was done, there was no going back.

×o×o×o

CHAPTER 11: DEAL WITH THE DEVIL

Juliet "Jules" Montclair

The moment I entered my room, I knew something was off.

It was a sensation first—a creeping, tingling wrongness tracing over my skin, settling into my bones. The kind of wrong that wasn't immediately apparent at a glance but seeped in like the reverberation of a crash, waiting for me to catch up.

I headed towards my vanity, already fumbling for my phone. Only—

It wasn't there.

The silk robe that I'd tossed across the chair remained undisturbed. The perfume bottles in their usual alignment, just as I'd left them. But my phone—vanished.

Not on my vanity. Not under the heap of silk and lace that I'd shed as I made my way into the shower. I rummaged through my bag, the pockets of my leather jacket, even the space on the floor in front of my bed as if somehow it could have dropped there. Nothing.

A slow, suffocating dread curled in my stomach.

Where had I left it?

I turned in a tight circle, scanning the room again, but the answer was already forming, crawling into my head like smoke. The race.

My head flashed back, reliving every moment that now mattered too much. The tense air, the smell of gas heavy in the darkness, motors purring like war drums under city lights. And more than that—Romy.

The way he'd looked at me.

Not just the manner of boys generally, as if I were something to be won. It wasn't the usual hunger, the following of my mouth with his eyes down to my thighs, the unspoken invitation. This was different. Tense. Plotted. Like he was seeking something.

I recalled then. The conversation.

Him, propped against the bumper of his car, the sneer nearly persuasive enough to not be fake. The way he touched my wrist with his fingertips when he put the wrench into my hand. A question, careless. Far too careless.

"How does somewhere like the Montclair showroom lock up at all? I mean, they don't give them out to just anyone, right?"

I'd laughed. Waved him off. "It's all controlled from my phone, anyway. I override everything."

No.

A chill, yawning void opened inside me, and for the first time in years, I felt it—fear. Real, gut-clenching fear. Not of my father. Not of scandal. Not of the expectations around my neck like a noose.

But of Romy.

Of what I already knew he'd done.

I grabbed my keys and fled.

By the time I arrived at the showroom, it was too late.

The lot was awash in dazzling white from the overhead floodlights, making the shiny cars act like mirrors, reflecting a sight I didn't want to believe was happening.

Romy remained in the center of it all, hands behind his back cuffed, head bent just so to cover his face. His shirt was ripped at the neckline, smeared with something black—grease, perhaps. Blood, perhaps. Two officers in uniforms stood beside him, holding tight as they pushed him toward the rear of one of their squad cars.

I couldn't breathe for an instant.

Then I ran.

Bulldozing through crowds, shoving through the thick smell of gasoline and scorched rubber, my heart racing in my throat. "Romy!"

Someone jerked me back. Hard.

"Not tonight, Princess."

Tyson.

His fingers dug into my arm, holding me in place. But it wasn't the hold that put my teeth on edge. It was the expression in his eyes. Smug. Self-satisfied. Like he'd been waiting for this moment, like he'd planned the whole damn thing.

I pulled away, chest heaving. "What the hell happened?"

Tyson exhaled slowly, deliberately, as if bored. As if my fear was a nuisance. "The Cruzers attempted to break-in to the showroom. I arrived just in time to prevent it."

"Bullshit." My tone cut through the air, trembling. "Romy wouldn't—"

But already, I'd remembered my phone. The way he'd tracked me at the race, the ease with which I'd provided him with every shred of information he required.

Tyson grinned. "Wouldn't he?"

Something passed between us—victory in his eyes, uncertainty in mine. He pulled out something small from his pocket, something that made my stomach drop.

My phone.

"Found this," he said, flinging it at me like garbage. "Must've dropped it."

I caught it, fingers closing hard around the icy metal edges. My heart pounded so hard it drowned out every logical thought.

"You set him up." The charge seared on my tongue, bitter and toxic.

Tyson shrugged. "You really think I had to?" He leaned in, lowering his voice. "You already knew what he was, Jules. A Cruzer. A thief. They take what they want and leave people like us in the ruins."

I wanted to shove him. Scream. Something. But my hands stayed clenched around my phone, nails biting into my palm.

"You're a liar."

"Am I?" His grin widened. "He stole my Ferrari, remember?"

I stilled.

Because that was the bad part. I had known. And I'd not cared.

Tyson regarded me, cocking his head as if he were examining the lines developing in my determination. "Wake up, Jules. The Cruzers? They're just what your dad's always claimed they were."

My throat shut.

I needed to fight. Needed to push him away, make him tell me what, make this better. But I didn't.

Because suddenly I wasn't so sure that I even had that right.

The engine of the squad car started up.

And I just stood there. And watched.

As he walked away.

Later, I attempted to visit Romy.

The station smelled like stale coffee and bad decisions, the kind that clung to your skin and didn't wash off. The officer behind the front desk barely looked up when I asked for him, his fingers still tapping against his keyboard listlessly as if my request wasn't even worthy of recognition.

"He doesn't want to see you," he said, flat.

Like being punched in the ribs. Like the earth beneath my feet dropping away.

I came close to laughing—because Romy was stubborn, because Romy would rather burn himself alive than acknowledge he needed assistance—but the look the officer gave me said it all I already knew. This was not Romy being obstinate. This was Romy excluding me.

I waited anyway. I sat in the waiting room, spine straight, fists clenched around the strap on my bag. The fluorescent lights hummed above, bathing everything in a cold, dead sheen. Men in shoddy suits and half-sleeping eyes passed by without glancing, and the clock on the wall crawled, as if taunting me.

When Detective Harris finally emerged, he didn't even register shock at seeing me. Just, resigned.

"Go home, Miss Montclair."

I raised my chin. "He didn't do this."

Harris exhaled as if he'd heard it all before, as if he'd sat a hundred girls like me in this chair, attempting to change a narrative already set.

"Walk away while you still can," he said.

I went away.

But I didn't walk away.

I unraveled.

Not in front of people—never in front of people. But in my room, in quiet, it caught up with me.

The betrayal. The uncertainty. The horrific, turning question: Was I the one to ruin him?

I filled the bath, cranked the water to scalding, and slipped under, letting the heat bite into my flesh.

I floated for a long time.

I could sink, I thought.

Just let go. Stop resisting. Let the weight drag me down.

Then a voice. Hard. Unrelenting. Cutting through the steam like a knife.

"Juliet."

Nia.

She was in the doorway, arms folded, her easy confidence marred by something darker. Something threatening.

"Ne les laisse pas te briser." Don't let them break you.

I didn't respond. Didn't budge.

She crossed the room, kneeling beside the tub, the tile cool beneath her knees. Then she reached into her pocket and retrieved her phone.

"I need you to listen."

A click. And then voices.

My father's. "Make sure Marco takes the bait."

Tyson's. "He'll tell Romy it's a clean job. You get what you need. I take care of the rest."

My gut went cold.

I gazed at Nia, the tone of their voices coiling into something raw and intolerable in my ears.

What is this? I thought. But I knew already.

She didn't wince. "Your father and Tyson framed Romy."

The air left my body.

No. No, no, no.

But the recording continued to play, their voices cementing my worst fear into reality. The fragments falling into place like broken glass reassembling a shattered frame.

I sat bolt upright, water spilling over the rim, saturating the floor. My heart thudded like a war drum.

"Where did you find this?" My voice was raw, barely audible.

Nia's face softened—just a little. "Est-ce que ça a de l'importance?" Does it matter?

No.

Because I was already on the move.

My father stood waiting when I strode into his study, clad in my bathrobe, in bare feet, still dripping water onto his newly polished floors.

He barely lifted his eyes from his desk. "That's quite an entrance, Juliet."

I threw my phone down on his desk. The audio

file was still up, my breath still short from playing it again and again until the words cut themselves into my bones.

"Framed him."

His lips curled. Not a smile, exactly—something icier. "You're angry." He steepled his fingers, completely unconcerned. "You'll see things differently tomorrow."

I ground my fingers into the lip of his desk, holding on so hard my knuckles hurt. "You used me," I said, shaking, low voice. "Used my ignorance." I pushed the words through the gap in my throat. "And now you're going to make it right."

He groaned like I was some especially stodgy board meeting. And then, after a long pause, he leaned over and took out his own phone, pressed the screen, and held it out to me.

My blood chilled.

A video.

Romy and I. That night, after the race. The way he'd dragged me in close, the way I'd kissed him as if the world was about to end.

And now it was.

Victor Montclair took a deep breath, measured. "The law is a merciless thing, Juliet. All the more so for individuals like your… unfortunate friend." He placed the phone on the counter, folding his hands once more like a judge sentencing a king. "Grand theft auto. You do know the charges, don't you?"

I gulped.

He went on, voice honey-smooth over steel. "Despite the fact that he's seventeen, the courts will indict him as an adult. Count on it." A pause, calculated. "And when they do, he'll never get out of those walls again. Not until he dies."

It was a blow to the ribcage.

He was saying exactly how this would go down.

Unless.

I forced my nails into my palms. "What do you want?"

My father smiled. Not like he was pleased—like he had already won.

"So here's what's going to happen, Juliet. You will stop racing. You will fall in line." He leaned back, like the outcome had never been in question. "And in return, I will ensure the charges against your… mistake of a summer disappear."

A choice.

But not really.

Because there wasn't a choice, was there?

I tilted my chin, gulped down the fire in my throat, and stared at him straight on. "Fine."

His lips twitched. "Good decision."

I whirled around before he could witness the tears stinging my eyes.

Because I wasn't crying for myself.

I was crying for Romy.

For the boy I loved.

The boy I'd just sold my soul to protect.

XoXoXo

CHAPTER 12: A TALE OF TWO HEARTBREAKS

Romeo "Romy" Cruzer

The heist was set in motion.

I shouldn't have been there.

But that was the thing about family—you didn't get to pick and choose when you belonged. You carried their sins like a second skin, wore their choices like hand-me-downs that never fit right. And when the time came, you stepped up.

Even when it burned.

The Montclair showroom stood silent under the

sickly glow of streetlights, a temple to power and greed. The glass gleamed, polished to perfection, every car inside worth more than my entire damn life.

Inside the van, Marco bounced his knee, his gold ring tapping against the seat. "We doing this or what?"

"We wait for Romy's signal," Tino muttered, rubbing a thumb over his chain. "We don't go in blind."

Uncle Rafa snorted, sliding a round into his gun like we were gearing up for war. Maybe we were.

Raul, my father, didn't say a word. He just watched. Silent approval. Silent expectation.

I swallowed the gravel in my throat and pulled out my phone.

Jules' phone.

A bad idea. A mistake. A thousand shades of wrong.

I tapped into the showroom's system, rerouting the security feed with the code I stole off her texts. My fingers felt slow. Hesitant. I told myself it wasn't because of her.

"Clear," I said, voice steady. A lie.

I stepped out first. Alone.

The night smelled like gasoline and rain—like something on the verge of burning. I pushed through the showroom doors, the silence swallowing me whole.

Too quiet.

I moved fast, scanning the rows of gleaming cars, my pulse hammering against my ribs. We had a clean two minutes before the guards made their next round.

Then the lights flicked on.

And I saw him.

Tyson Vega.

Leaning against the hood of a jet-black Porsche, all smirk and venom, arms folded like he'd been waiting just for me.

"Didn't think you'd actually be stupid enough to show up," he mused. "But then again, you always were an overconfident little shit."

I went cold. The kind of cold that seeped into your bones, slow and deadly.

Tyson. Jules' cousin.

My hands curled into fists. "I don't know what the hell you think you're doing, Tyson, but you don't want this fight."

He tilted his head, like I was some kind of

fascinating problem he had all the time in the world to solve. "Oh, I do, actually."

The sirens wailed in the distance.

Not far.

Not enough time.

"You don't try anything," Tyson said, his voice a razor against my skin. "You don't run. You don't call your little family waiting outside, because if they're caught?" His smirk deepened. "Well, then all of the Cruzers can spend family days inside prison."

The words hit harder than a punch.

He knew.

He had always known.

And I had walked right into his trap.

I spun, sprinting for the exit, but it was already too late—red and blue lights bled through the glass, the heavy slam of car doors, voices barking orders.

The glass doors burst open, and I barely had time to lift my hands before they shoved me down.

Knees in my back. A gun to my head.

Handcuffs biting into my wrists.

I barely heard the Miranda rights over the ringing in my ears.

I only heard one thing—Tyson's voice, low and smug.

"See you in hell, Cruzer."

The steel of the cuffs burned against my skin.

The air outside was thick—humid, choking. I barely registered the flashing lights, the sea of uniformed cops, the cameras already swarming in like vultures.

I kept my head down.

Then I heard her.

"Romy—"

Jules.

I flinched before I even saw her.

She was running toward me, shoving past the cops, barefoot like she'd come straight from bed. The look on her face—raw, desperate—made something twist in my ribs.

I couldn't do this.

I turned away, shoving myself into the backseat of the patrol car before I could see whatever was written in her eyes.

The door slammed shut.

I stared straight ahead as they drove me away.

The cell walls smelled like piss and sweat.

Like regret soaked into concrete. Like every bad decision that led to this moment.

A buzzing light flickered overhead, throwing shadows across the bars, stretching them long and thin, like the ribs of some starving animal. The air was stale, thick with the weight of too many stories ending the same way.

I sat on the edge of the cot, elbows on my knees, head in my hands, listening. Not to the silence—there was never real silence in a place like this. Just the distant shuffle of footsteps. The hollow clinking of metal. The quiet, muffled weeping of some kid in the next cell over, the sound of lives being dragged through the dirt.

My wrists still ached from the cuffs. Red marks, skin broken where the metal bit deep. My heartbeat felt slow, dull, like a car idling in the cold.

The lawyer came. Not my lawyer. Just some half-bored, underpaid suit they sent to pretend I had a chance. He looked at me like he'd already written me off, like he was calculating how much time he'd have to spend on this case before moving on to someone who could actually pay him.

"The prosecution is pushing for adult charges," he said, flipping open a folder like it contained something worse than my own future.

I exhaled slow, pressing my palms together, feeling my nails bite into my skin.

Seventeen.

They were gonna bury me before I even turned eighteen.

"You're looking at grand theft auto, breaking and entering, conspiracy. A lot of moving pieces, Romeo." His voice was monotone, like he wasn't gutting me open with every word. "If they can pin gang affiliation on you—"

I laughed. Short. Ugly. "Gang affiliation?"

His eyes flicked up from the folder. "They'll argue the Cruzers are organized crime."

"They're my family."

He sighed like I was an idiot. Maybe I was. "Yeah. That's what makes this worse."

He kept talking. Something about plea deals. About trials and minimum sentencing. But the words blurred, melting into the walls, into the sound of my own breathing. My heartbeat wasn't slow anymore. It was fucking pounding.

I looked at my hands. Thought of my dad. Thought of my brothers, probably still sitting in the holding cells down the hall, waiting to hear if we'd all go down together or if one of us would flip first.

The lawyer stood. "I'll be back tomorrow."

I didn't answer.

The guard showed up next, leaning against the bars like he had all the time in the world.

"You got a visitor."

I didn't ask who. Didn't have to.

Jules.

For a second, something moved in my chest, sharp and raw.

And then I buried it.

I stared at the wall. "Not seeing anyone."

The guard shrugged. "Suit yourself."

Footsteps. The sound of a door opening. Closing.

And then nothing.

I sat there, breathing through my teeth, jaw clenched so tight it ached.

Jules.

Of course, she came.

And for the first time since the sirens, since the cuffs, since the moment I knew I was well and truly fucked—I felt something close to fear.

Because if I saw her now?

I wouldn't have the strength to send her away.

And that?

That would ruin us both.

The TV outside the cell was too loud.

Didn't matter that I wasn't watching. The words slithered through the bars anyway, sinking their teeth in.

A press conference.

I already knew what was coming before I heard the name. Before the camera cut to the podium. Before the world stopped turning.

The Montclairs.

My stomach was already tight, twisted, bracing. But nothing could've prepared me for what I heard next.

Jules' voice.

Clear. Cool. Devoid of everything that had ever been us.

"I didn't know who he really was."

"I was manipulated."

"He used me to steal from my family."

The world tilted.

No.

No, no, no.

The breath punched out of me as I forced myself to look.

She was standing at that podium, her father at her side, every camera on her. Her face was unreadable. Perfectly curated. Untouchable.

Like I'd never been there at all.

Like I wasn't rotting in a six-by-eight cell while she stood there and called me a criminal.

Like she hadn't told me she loved me.

Something cracked in my chest.

The ache crawled up my throat, something thick and ugly, but I swallowed it down, burying it somewhere deep and dark.

That was it, then.

Jules Montclair had just put the final nail in my coffin.

And this time, there was no getting out.

Laughter. A low whistle.

"Damn, kid."

I blinked, realizing suddenly that I wasn't alone.

The other officers had gathered around the TV, leaning against desks, arms crossed, watching the press conference like it was the season finale of their favorite crime drama.

One of them—a broad-shouldered guy with a scar on his jaw—tilted his head at me. "She really did you dirty, huh?"

I didn't answer. Didn't even look at him.

Another one chuckled. "Guess she found out what you really are, Cruzer."

I clenched my jaw so tight my teeth ached.

I wasn't gonna give them a show.

I wasn't gonna let them see how deep it cut, how my whole body felt like it was unraveling from the inside out.

I turned back to the wall.

But even with my eyes closed, I still saw her.

Still heard her voice.

Still felt the ghost of her fingertips against my skin, the way she used to whisper my name like it was something worth saying.

But that was a lifetime ago.

Before the sirens.

Before the handcuffs.

Before the girl I loved buried me alive.

xoxoxo

CHAPTER 13: SIGNALS IN THE NOISE

Juliet "Jules" Montclair

Tyson tapped a manicured finger against the glass table, watching me like a man studying a caged animal, waiting to see if I'd bite.

"Say it again."

I exhaled through my nose, my jaw locked. "I didn't know who he really was."

He sighed. "Jules, darling, you're not reciting a grocery list." He leaned forward, sharp-eyed and smug. "Again. Make them believe you."

I ground my teeth, pulse pounding. "I didn't know who he really was."

Tyson clicked his tongue. "Too stiff. No one's going to buy it if you sound like a hostage."

I wanted to tell him that's exactly what I was.

The PR training had gone on forever, his words pounding in my head like a metronome. He instructed me in tilting my head at precisely the correct angle, allowing my voice to shake—not too hard, just enough. How to spin a lie so convincingly it would wrap itself around me like silk.

How to villainize Romy.

How to victimize myself.

Tyson stood, pacing behind me like a professor with a struggling student. "You have to understand something, Jules." He stopped, hands resting on the back of my chair, his voice silk and steel. "This isn't about saving face. This is about living."

I didn't blink. But my fists curled in my lap.

Do you know what you get if you slip?" he whispered, standing too close. "If they suspect, for a moment, that you are lying? That you knew it all along?"

I didn't reply.

His fingers drummed against the arm of the chair. "Your father loses his reputation. Your dead mother's name is dragged in the dirt. Every Montclair investment is hit. And you?" His smile twisted, all teeth, no warmth. "You become the family's greatest failure.

I gulped, my throat parched.

"You're a Montclair, Jules," he went on, his voice gentler now, almost comforting. "We don't break. We don't bend. We erase the things that can hurt us before they have the chance."

I gritted my teeth, holding my voice firm. "Romy isn't a thing."

Tyson grinned, his hand on my shoulder in a light tap. "Not after tonight."

I took a deep, careful breath, watching my own reflection stare back at me from the glass tabletop.

He was not wrong about anything.

This press conference was more than damage control.

It was a funeral.

And I was preparing to bury the only boy I ever

loved.

The podium acted like a guillotine.

A shiny, mahogany block of execution where I stood, perfect and poised, as the world waited for me to get on with it. Harsh lights blazed down from all angles, bathing me in some yellow, some fake-looking—like I wasn't human, just another Montclair PR media event. Cameras popped in staccato flashes, their light cutting through the air, breaking everything into a jerky slideshow.

Beside me, my father exuded authority, hand hovering at the curve of my spine. Barely perceptible, so nobody would suspect. Solid enough I would know that this was where my body ought to stay.

I sensed the pressure of their hopes against me. The Langfords. The Montclairs. Everybody.

The same stifling pressure I had always known—wear the proper dress, sit upright, be a Montclair by name, by bearing, by each savagely chiseled inch of my being. And now, be the scorned girl. The sad heiress who had been swept off her feet by a felon and betrayed in the worst possible manner.

But Romy wasn't a felon.

And I wasn't the victim they required me to be.

I found the printed speech on the podium where Tyson had left it, but I didn't have to read it. I had spent hours trapped in a conference room with him repeating these words over and over again in my head, rehearsing the pauses, the precise angle at which to drop my eyes, the exact moment to add the slightest shake to my voice. It had been honed to a science.

I raised my chin, staring directly into the cameras.

"I didn't know who he really was."

The words felt like metal, like blood in my mouth.

The room was quiet except for the sound of cameras clicking and the soft hum of reporters scribbling things down. In the crowd, I caught a glimpse of a woman pressing a sympathetic hand to her chest, as if I was shattering her heart. I almost laughed.

"I was manipulated."

My cheek twitched with a muscle, and I calmed it away before it became something actual. This had nothing to do with me. This had everything to do with the Montclair name.

It had everything to do with putting Romy in the ground.

"He used me to steal from my family."

My hands wrapped around the podium so hard my nails burrowed into the wood. The last words flew off my lips, cold as glass, and left something shattered behind.

A silence fell. Not the anxious one. The funeral sort.

I didn't need to look at the TV screens to be certain that Romy was watching somewhere inside that jail.

I didn't need to look at his face to be certain I had just broken something between us.

Perhaps forever.

The Langfords' manor dinner was worse too. Their dining room smelled of old wine and old cash.

Polished silver, Baccarat crystal, the soft hum of voices shrouded in thinly veiled condescension—it was a scene I had lived a hundred times before. A stage where the players dressed in designer suits and empty smiles, where love was an artful performance, nothing more.

Dominic Langford's mother leaned her head in my direction, her pearls gliding against her neck.

"Juliet, sweetie, you have to be so thrilled about next season's charity gala. Naturally, we'll have you included—you'll be such a pretty face for the foundation." I smiled politely, the kind that didn't touch my eyes. "Of course. It sounds. lovely."

"Oh, and we simply must get you into The Argyle Women's Society—it's such an exclusive circle. You'll love it."

Love it. Sure. Just like I loved every crushing expectation they stamped into my flesh like a brand.

Dominic observed me across the table, his face inscrutable as he stirred his whiskey. Silent. Removed. The ideal Langford heir.

My father, ever the picture of effortless power, took his time finishing his wine before setting the glass down with a deliberate, measured finality.

The air in the room shifted.

"We've decided on the engagement," he said smoothly. "Dominic and Juliet will be officially announced as a couple at her birthday celebration in two weeks."

A simple statement, absolute in its certainty.

My pulse roared in my ears.

As if my life was another corporate takeover.

There was no shock in Dominic's expression. No flutter of uncertainty. He didn't even blink, just kept stirring the amber drink in his glass as if all this was predestined.

Because it was.

The Langfords shared glances, their assent silent but clear. His mother laid a cool, delicate hand over mine, glass-skin fragile. "We couldn't be more delighted, dear. You and Dominic will be just right for each other."

I hardly registered her touch.

"Let's raise a glass," Dominic's father announced, raising his glass. Crystal stemware around the table reflected the candlelight, an icy, heartless spectacle.

"To the new Mr. and Mrs. Langford."

The words hit like a blade between my ribs.

I set my fork down carefully, steady despite the storm in my chest. "I'm not agreeing to this."

A sharp silence fell, but my father's smile didn't waver.

"You don't need to."

It was like being locked in a cage with invisible

bars.

The Langfords exchanged polite glances, unfazed, as if my defiance was no more than an inconvenience—a minor wrinkle in an otherwise perfect plan.

I pushed back my chair, the scrape of it against marble slicing through the silence. "Excuse me."

No one stopped me.

Not even Dominic.

But the car ride back home with my father was no better.

The silence in the back of the Bentley was thick enough to drown in.

Outside, Toronto whizzed by in a blur of neon glints through the tinted glass—gold and blue and red smearing across the surface like some kind of impressionist delirium. The pressure of the night pushed against my ribs, choking in a manner that no silk gown or gleaming diamond could dispel.

I spoke to my father. "You promised something to me."

He didn't glance at me immediately. Instead, his fingers drummed idly against his knee—accurate, calculated, as if he were tapping out the beat to a tune he heard alone. "I've promised you much."

I balled my fists in my lap, nails sinking into the meat of my palm. "You said you'd release Romy."

That caught his attention. A flick of his eye, detached and cool, as if I were a child reminding him of a bedtime tale he'd long forgotten. "And I have."

I breathed sharply. "Then make it official. Drop the charges."

He turned his head to regard me in a way I felt like he would regard an especially dull business proposal. "If I do," he moved slowly, thinking, "you will be good. No scandal. No acts of folly. No—" He exhaled fast, decisively. "Romeo Cruzer."

His voice cut between us like a knife, intentional in its directness.

Romy was not a human being to him. Just another hassle. A variable in a precisely controlled formula that my father would not allow to descend into anarchy.

I did not wince, did not allow him to see the way my pulse pounded against my neck. "Fine."

He looked at me for another second before he nodded.

Then, with a silent efficiency that curled my stomach, he got out his phone and called. A few words were spoken, curt and impersonal. And in an instant, Romy was free.

Just like that, I wasn't.

I leaned against the cold glass, my forehead against it, as the city lights flashed by.

He spoke again, voice smooth as cut marble. "You'll be ready for the engagement party. I've hired people for it."

Of course, he had.

It wasn't about the party. It wasn't even about the dress fittings or the public spectacle. It was about keeping me occupied, keeping me watched. Every second accounted for, every move predicted.

A leash disguised as luxury.

I breathed out, slow and quiet, as the car curved onto the private drive leading to our estate.

I had bought Romy's freedom with the last of my own.

But the engagement preparations were hell.

They stripped me down to bare skin and expectation, at any rate.

Not literally, though it might as well have been.

The days ran together in a blur of beauty treatments, posture exercises, constant fittings. I posed before mirrors as strangers I hardly knew adjusted my form like a mannequin, their hands cool and impersonal as they smoothed silk over my flesh and pinned diamonds against my collarbone. A sculpted mask, honed until I was lost beneath it.

"Smile, but don't show too many teeth."

"Walk like a Montclair."

"Hold your fiancé's arm like you love him, even if you don't."

Every command was another strand in the chain around my ribs, cinching with each breath.

Dominic Langford observed it all in quiet detachment.

He was always there, hovering around the periphery of the performance, a smooth statue in a sleekly tailored suit. Let them pin me to his side, let them pose us in posed affection. His hand on my waist, my hand resting lightly on his forearm. He never touched me for more time than he had to. Never gazed at me for longer than was required.

I wondered whether that was his own act of defiance.

It was just another rehearsal and we were alone in one of the estate's ballrooms—practicing the way he was to hold me for our first dance.

It was a stage, essentially. Chandelier light off gold-edged ceilings, shadows cast across marble floors.

Dominic's hold was firm but unpersonal, walking me through the motions with a precision that seemed more duty than anything else.

"Does it bother you?" I said, the words tumbling out before I could catch them.

He didn't flinch. "Does what bother me?"

"Marrying a girl who doesn't love you.

For the first time, something flashed behind his otherwise impenetrable face. A fissure in the smooth glass. It was over before I could read it.

His lips curled only slightly. "It's no better than marrying someone who loves another."

I gasped, the impact of his words hanging between us.

He didn't lie.

We both knew the truth.

That didn't mean it mattered.

But I stole minutes where I could.

A few moments of silence between fittings, when the seamstresses turned their backs. A few gasps of air on the balcony, frigid air cutting through the scented evening.

Planning. Laying out plans. Practicing escape routes in my mind.

They believed they had me under wraps. That every step was tracked, every breath weighed. They didn't know that deep down, behind the gleaming facade, I was still ablaze.

And then, the news.

It flashed on my phone screen in stark, clinical letters—*Accused car thief Romeo Cruzer makes bail.*

My heart skipped a beat. A delayed response, like the instant before the crash. Then it surged, a mad, out-of-control thing trying to burst out of my heart.

I read the words until they ran together. Until I could catch my breath.

Romy was free. At least for now.

And that should have sufficed.

But it didn't.

Because I had one more thing to do.

My garage still reeked of oil and adrenaline, though I hadn't been racing in weeks. I was kept on a short leash now, they had my wings clipped so neatly it almost resembled obedience.

Almost.

I pulled the tarp back, showing the car Romy once told me suited me better than my pearls. Sleek, deadly, designed to outrun expectations.

My fingers trembled as I ripped out a page from an old maintenance log and scratched the message in the only ink that felt true—smudged grease and gasoline along the margins.

"If you ever need to run, find me at the finish line."

The place where we weren't a Montclair and a Cruzer.

Where we were merely two people, chasing something impossible.

XoXoXo

CHAPTER 14: THE ESCAPE PLAN

Romeo "Romy" Cruzer

Bail didn't mean freedom.

It meant walking out of one kind of prison and straight into another.

The moment I stepped through the shop doors, I knew. Knew it from the way my father wouldn't meet my eyes, the way my mother wrung her hands like she was praying for me, the way my uncle Rafa sat with his arms folded, face carved from stone.

And Marco.

Marco stood there with that same easy smirk he

always wore when he was about to ruin someone's life, like what he was about to say was just another joke, just another game.

"Heard you dropped out of school," he said, flicking a cigarette into the oil-stained pavement. "Before summer even started. Thought you were better at keeping secrets, cousin."

The silence that followed cracked like a gunshot. Marco had thrown me under the bus, literally.

I kept my face blank, but inside, something twisted sharp. My family finding out about Jules? That was inevitable. But dropping out? That was my own mistake, one I'd been keeping under wraps for months.

Raul Cruzer didn't yell. He didn't throw things. He didn't even curse. He just exhaled, slow and sharp, like the weight of my failure had just settled onto his back.

"So you really thought," he murmured, "you could just run around with a Montclair and it wouldn't come back to us?"

"Jules isn't—"

Uncle Rafa cut me off.

"Juliet Montclair is getting engaged," he said, voice as smooth as the edge of a blade. "To Dominic

Langford."

My stomach bottomed out.

Marco watched me, waiting for the reaction, waiting to see if I'd flinch. I didn't.

Of course, she was. It was only a matter of time.

"You got played, cuz," Marco said, shaking his head. "You really thought a Montclair would fall for a Cruzer? That she'd pick some street racer over a Langford? Shit, man, you're dumber than I thought."

I clenched my fists. "You don't know her."

"Oh, but you do?" Marco laughed, a harsh sound that scraped against my nerves. "Face it, Romy. She used you. She's the reason you're standing here like a stray dog, waiting to get kicked out."

"You're one to talk, *snitch*," I spat, stepping closer. "Selling me out to my own family? What, that make you feel big?"

Marco's smirk vanished. "You did that to yourself. You're the one getting too close to the enemy."

"She's not the enemy."

"She's a Montclair, and that's all that fucking matters."

I hit him before I even realized I was moving. A

clean, brutal punch to the jaw that sent him stumbling back against a metal workbench, tools rattling as he caught himself. He wiped his mouth, blinking at the blood on his fingers before letting out a dry, humorless laugh.

"That all you got?" Marco taunted, rolling his jaw. "Pathetic."

I didn't give him the satisfaction of a response. Just stood there, my breath coming sharp and fast, my hand aching from the hit.

My father rose from his chair, turning his back on me. A dismissal. My mother moved toward me, but he stopped her with a look.

"You're not my son anymore," he said.

It was quiet. Just four words. But they cracked something inside me, something I wasn't sure would ever fix itself.

I swallowed hard, forcing myself to nod. "Yeah. I figured."

I turned and walked out before I could give them the satisfaction of seeing me break.

No home. No family. No name.

Just me. And whatever came next.

Toronto's underground scene was different when you had nothing.

When you had a home, you moved through the city like it was yours—glass towers reflecting the sky, streets humming with people who had places to be, things to lose. But when you had nothing, the city turned on you. The lights were too bright, too sharp. The streets stretched longer, colder. The world didn't slow down for people like me. It swallowed us whole.

I crashed where I could. Slept in the back of gutted cars, on stained mattresses in garages where the air reeked of oil and desperation. I learned which shelters kept their doors open late, which back alleys had awnings deep enough to keep the rain off. The underground had its own set of rules—keep your head down, your mouth shut, and if someone hands you an opportunity, take it before it disappears.

I ran with guys I used to race against. Spent nights in chop shops, trading work for a place to crash, eating whatever scraps someone shoved my way. Some nights, I'd find my way to the underpass, where the real ghosts of the city gathered—kids younger than me, faces hollowed out by hunger and things they wouldn't talk about. You learned quick. The ones who hesitated, who still carried softness in their bones—they didn't last.

There were nights I woke up to screaming in alleyways, sirens swallowing the city whole. Nights I kept my hand in my pocket, fingers wrapped around the cool weight of a switchblade, just in case. I wasn't looking for trouble, but I wasn't stupid enough to think it wasn't looking for me.

I was nothing. No name. No family. Just another ghost moving through the city, waiting to disappear.

And then Jules found me.

She didn't belong here. Not in the underground garages where the stink of gasoline mixed with the acrid burn of cheap cigarettes. Not in this world where survival was a game of who could bleed the least. But there she was—standing under the flickering neon glow of a busted streetlamp, hood pulled up, hands shoved deep in the pockets of an oversized hoodie that still couldn't hide the way she carried herself. Too clean. Too careful. Too hers.

I lit a cigarette just to keep my hands from shaking. The lighter's click was too loud in the silence stretching between us.

"Thought I was done with Montclairs," I muttered, exhaling smoke between us like a shield.

Jules snorted, but the sound was hollow. "Thought I was done with Cruzers."

Almost made me smile. Almost.

Then I saw it—the barely-there tremor in her fingers, the tightness in her jaw, the way she kept glancing over her shoulder like she was waiting for a bullet. For a ghost. For something worse.

"He followed me."

Two words. That was all it took for my stomach to drop like a dead weight.

Tyson.

That snake had been on my ass since the first time I touched Jules. The Montclairs' enforcer, her father's right hand, the kind of guy who didn't need to raise his voice to send a message. He'd killed men for less than what I'd done with his boss's daughter.

I rolled my shoulders back, feigning indifference even as my pulse kicked up. "Yeah? And?"

"And he's watching us. Right now."

My fingers curled around the cigarette. I didn't

turn, didn't give Tyson the satisfaction of knowing I gave a damn.

"You're engaged," I said instead. Voice flat. Cold. Like I didn't care. Like it wasn't a knife between my ribs.

Jules flinched. Just barely. "Not by choice."

"Yeah? That supposed to make it better?"

Her throat worked as she swallowed hard. "It's complicated."

"It's not," I said, flicking ash onto the pavement. "You belong to him now. That's all there is."

She sucked in a breath, but I didn't let her answer. Didn't let myself look too long at the way her eyes shone under the streetlights. Didn't let myself wonder if it was tears or anger.

"Are you serious right now?" she snapped, voice rising, words laced with something venomous. "You actually think I wanted to see you again?"

It hit harder than I expected.

I forced a laugh, cruel and empty. "Right. Guess you just missed slumming it with the criminals."

Her jaw clenched. She shoved me, hard, catching me off guard, making me stumble back a step.

"You were never supposed to be more than a summer fling," she hissed.

I saw it then. The way her pupils blew wide. The way her chest rose and fell too fast. The way she refused to break eye contact like she was daring me to call her bluff.

Read between the lines, Romy.

She was putting on a show.

For Tyson.

For whoever else was watching.

My hands curled into fists. "Then get the hell out of here, princess."

Her lips parted—like maybe she wanted to say something else. Like maybe she wanted to tell me the truth. But instead, she turned on her heel, storming off like she meant it, like she'd won.

And as she passed, her hand brushed mine. Just for a second. Just long enough.

A scrap of paper pressed into my palm.

I didn't have to look to know what it said.

"If you ever need to run, find me at the finish line."

The words sat heavy in my chest, pressing against something raw, something I had tried to bury beneath weeks of distance and unspoken things.

She still loved me.

And then—before I could even process what it meant—it was Marco who reached out first.

The burner phone vibrated in my pocket, a number I knew by heart but hadn't seen on my screen since the night I walked out. Since the night my father's voice turned to steel and my name stopped meaning home.

I almost let it ring out. Almost. But I answered, pressing the phone to my ear, listening to the familiar static of Marco's car stereo in the background. He was driving. Probably circling the block, trying to decide if this call was worth the risk.

"So, you finally grew a brain," Marco said, voice dry. "Or just ran out of places to crash?"

I leaned against the driver seat. "Need some cash."

He snorted. "No shit. That why you called?"

"You called me."

A pause. The sound of him taking a drag off a cigarette, exhaling slow. "The family is willing to forgive you, you know. But you gotta be smart about this. No more Montclairs, no more bullshit."

I closed my eyes. "Not gonna happen."

Marco swore under his breath. "Jesus, Romy. You really don't get it, do you?" His voice shifted, lower now, edged with something close to worry. "She's not one of us. And she never will be. You think she's gonna stick around when everything goes south?"

"You don't know her."

"Nah," he said, sharp and mean. "I know you. I know that when she leaves—and she will—you'll be nothing. Just like the rest of us."

I swallowed against the tightness in my throat. "Either help me, or don't."

"Fine." Marco let out a slow sigh. "You wanna burn your life down? Fine. Just don't say I didn't warn you."

I almost laughed at that. Almost.

Then the line went dead.

For a second, I just stood there, phone still in my hand, the weight of his words pressing against my ribs. Burn my life down? Like it wasn't already in ashes. Like I had anything left to lose.

But I still had one last race. One last score.

I told myself it wasn't about the money, but that

was a lie. The cash was the only way out. A fresh start, away from the Montclairs, away from my family's name burning a hole in my skin like a brand. Away from this city that had already decided how our story would end.

The air smelled like gasoline and bad decisions, neon lights flickering against sweat-slick pavement. Engines revved, the sound vibrating through my ribs. The crowd was thick, the kind of people who didn't ask questions, who only cared about the rush, the speed, the risk.

I flexed my fingers against the wheel, inhaled deep. This was the only place where my mind ever went quiet. Where there was nothing but me, the machine, and the road.

Someone knocked against my window. "You sure about this?"

"No."

He shook his head but stepped back anyway. "See you at the finish line."

The starter girl raised her arms. I revved the engine. Hands steady.

Didn't notice the shadows shifting at the edge of the crowd. Didn't see the setup coming.

The flag dropped.

And I gunned it into the night.

×o×o×o

CHAPTER 15: OUT OF CONTROL

Juliet "Jules" Montclair

Two days.

Forty-eight hours until my dad would trot me out before Toronto's upper class like a winning racehorse, a Montclair-stamped prize to be bound legally to Dominic Langford for the remainder of my life.

The wedding party had been planned for weeks—carefully timed to take place on the day of my eighteenth birthday. A seal of ownership. No longer a kid. No longer can say no. And by its end, the future would be cemented, signatures on documents, his surname tied to mine. A good match, it was what my father deemed so. A deal of inheritance. A combination. A dynasty formed.

I called it a prison sentence.

The Montclair estate was a whirl of activity. Event coordinators poured through the house, covering the marble floors in a never-ending cycle of flower arrangements and seating diagrams. The aroma of imported roses permeated the air, heavy and overpowering, choking. My mother's favorite. Or so my father said, although she'd been dead long enough that no one could dispute his carefully constructed recollections.

Designers flitted in and out in a blur of rotation, racks of lace and silk rolled through my bedroom like I was a doll to be dressed. Each morning, I faced the mirror while stylists argued over which tone of ivory was most flattering on my skin. As if it mattered. As if the color of my gown would somehow make me desire this.

The whole city was gearing up for the event. I was the only one who wasn't.

Tyson Vega, my cousin, the Montclair enforcer, was eyeing me like a hawk.

He was everywhere. Hanging in doorways. Standing over my shoulder. Sitting across from me at breakfast, arms folded, his espresso untouched. He didn't trust my sudden compliance. Didn't think, for a second, that I'd transformed from spitting fire to compliant heiress overnight.

And he was justified not to.

"So, what's the sudden change of heart?" Tyson asked me at last one afternoon, bracing himself in the doorframe of my room, arms crossed.

I didn't even bother to look up from my phone. "Maybe I've finally resigned myself to my destiny."

He snorted. "Yeah. And maybe I suddenly want to dress in pastels."

I sighed and threw my phone onto the bed. "What do you want, Tyson?"

"To know what the hell you're up to." He moved in, his voice dropping. "I've known you since we were kids. You're not the kind of girl to roll over. So what's changed?"

Nothing. And everything.

I gave him my most bored look. "Maybe I just got tired of fighting."

Tyson's eyes narrowed, suspicion wrapping around him like cigarette smoke. He didn't believe me. Not for a second. But he didn't have proof.

Not yet.

My go-bag was already packed, tucked behind layers of forgotten couture in the back of my closet. A museum of past versions of myself—ball gowns I'd worn once, designer pieces hand-selected by my father's stylists, dresses chosen not for me but for the image they created. A Montclair daughter. A future Langford wife.

But not me.

Hidden underneath the silk and sequins was my real escape. Clothes—ones I could actually run in. Money—enough to leave. A burner phone—because even a whisper could be traced in my world.

Romy and I had mapped it out in the wee hours of the night, our voices barely above a whisper, heavy with desperation. He whispered in low tones, his voice a live wire down the phone, coursing through my veins. We had one shot. One night.

Our smoke screen would be the engagement party. While the city looked on, while there were flashing cameras and champagne toasts, we'd make our escape. One last vanishing act. One final act of defiance.

But first, I had to get through one more farce.

The Montclair estate was ours for the night—a curated farewell to the life I was supposed to want. My father had agreed, allowing me to invite a few friends, as if this was some grand send-off before I donned the golden shackles of my engagement. A final indulgence before I became Dominic's perfect fiancée.

The house was filled with soft jazz and the tinkling of crystal, the kind of easy wealth that oozed from every gleaming surface. Beyond the glass, the city lay stretched out before us like a neon dream, lights flashing in the glass horizon. A world I had never really been a part of, however well I fit into my role.

The invitation list was deliberate—necessarily chosen names to match the future I was destined to inherit.

Leo Mercier, the heir to the fortune that had even my father take pause, sat next to me, regarding me as if I were something just beyond his grasp. Always waiting—hovering in the background, waiting. Not a Montclair by birth, but near enough. Near enough that people guessed, that my father had once seriously considered it.

Then there was Sara Lin, the daughter of a real estate mogul, the girl who had always played by the rules. She sat on the balcony ledge, ankles crossed at the knees. She was subdued tonight, swirling the champagne in her glass, fingers running around the rim as if she was hearing music that only she could hear.

I raised my own glass, the bubbles shining in the moonlight, and sipped slowly. "You need to quit staring at me like that," I whispered, not even bothering to turn toward Leo.

He blinked. "Like what?"

"Like you're waiting for something that's never going to occur."

His jaw clenched, his fingers closing around his drink. "Jules—"

"I know, Leo." I finally looked at him. "I've always known."

The quiet between us grew heavy as the summer

air, thick with all that he never actually spoke aloud.

His breathing caught, his composed mask cracking for a split moment. "You could have simply told me," he said in a low tone.

I blew out a breath, shaking my head before he could get anything else out. There was nothing to say. He knew, too. He just didn't want to ever say it.

Rather, I looked over at Sara, a few feet down from me, her eyes dreamy, running her thumb automatically over the drops of condensation on her drink. The expression she wore whenever she gazed at Leo as if no one was observing them. The manner in which she had always done so.

"Unrequited love is the worst feeling in the world," I told him, my tone airy. Then back to Leo, my head cocked. "But not for you."

His eyes furrowed. "What the hell do you mean by that?"

I tipped my chin in Sara's direction.

Leo tracked my stare. His brow furrowed as he looked at her, something unspoken falling into place, like a puzzle he'd refused to complete. The epiphany was slow, stretched out, but when it hit—when it really hit—I saw the change in his face.

I smiled, taking another sip of champagne. "You're an idiot, you know that?"

He didn't respond. Didn't have to.

A thread loosened. A tie broke free. And for the first time in a long time, I felt like I had done something right.

The party was beginning to wind down, the charge of electricity fading into the low buzz of near-empty conversation and the ring of champagne glasses. Outside, the Toronto skyline blazed like the broken shards of a dream that I had never desired. The air was scented with overpriced perfume, with something too good, too finished.

That was when I saw her.

Nia. The housekeeper.

She stood just at the edge of the big hall, her fingers wrapped around each other, her face pinched with haste. She wasn't where she was supposed to be— staff had better sense than to interrupt one of my father's well-planned events.

I moved forward. "Nia?"

Her voice was low, a warning infused with

desperate calm. "Juliet, your cousin—"

Too late.

The closet door burst open upstairs. Dresses—trains of silk and tulle, the leftover dresses of a girl I was no longer—were discarded. My go-bag sat on the floor, its neatly packed belongings spilled like evidence of my wrongdoing.

Tyson loomed over it, his eyes somber with something that wasn't anger. No, this was worse. This was disappointment, the kind that got into your bones and didn't leave.

"Where are you going?" He spoke low, deadly.

I said nothing. There was nothing to say.

His fingers wrapped hard around my wrist before I could step back. "You're going with me."

Leo reached for me, but Tyson hardly registered him, pushing him back with a single abrupt motion. "Out of this, Mercier."

Leo swore under his breath but didn't try again. He knew better. Tyson had always been stronger, always had the weight of our family name behind him.

I didn't fight. Not this time. Not because I'd lost the will to fight, but because I wanted to see my dad's expression when I said goodbye. When I tell him that I would never be coming home again.

The ride to my dad's showroom was smothering. The city swept by in a sheen of streetlights and glass towers, but I did not see them. Tyson drove the way he always drove—restrained, accurate, the good soldier my father had drilled into him.

"Why now, Jules?" His voice pierced the quiet, with something almost like regret. Almost.

I faced him, my face empty. "Because if I don't, I won't live."

He breathed sharply but didn't dispute. He knew I wasn't lying. He just didn't care enough to release me.

Victor Montclair was waiting.

He sat behind his mahogany desk, the empire he had forged mirrored in the glass walls surrounding him. The aroma of his cologne—a cold, woody scent that never smelled of home—filled the air.

Tyson pushed me forward.

"Juliet." My father sighed my name as if it were a burden.

"Father." My tone was firm. Unshakeable. I would not allow him to see me crack.

He sighed, shaking his head. "Why do you insist on making things difficult?"

I lifted my chin. "Why do you insist on ruining my life?"

He leaned in closer, his eyes scanning me as if I were a failed investment. "Do you think your mother would be proud of you right now?"

A knife in the ribs. An old pain.

My breath caught, but I kept my tone level. "She's not here."

"She would want what's best for you."

"You mean she would want what's best for you."

I understood what he was doing. He had always employed her memory as a leash, a chain to keep me bound to the life he had created for me. But my mom loved me. And if she had been alive, she never would have allowed him to make me into this—into a pawn in his never-ending game.

His patience grew thin. "You will marry Dominic. You will keep up the Montclair name. And you'll call off this childish rebellion before it hurts someone."

I glared at him, my heart slamming into my ribs. "I will never stop trying to escape. As long as I breathe."

"Very well then, you leave me no choice." His face twisted. "Tyson. Take care of it."

Tyson's grip on my wrist tightened, but this time he wasn't pulling me away. He was smiling. A slow, knowing smile.

He pulled out his phone, the screen lighting up against the dim light. He held it out to me. "You might want to rethink this, cousin."

I stood stock-still.

A live feed. Romy. At the starting line.

Tyson's voice was soft, mocking. "This is his last race." He let the words sink in, let the weight of them wrap around my throat like a noose. "Last chance to change your mind."

I met his gaze. "I'd rather die before that happens."

His smirk didn't falter. "Suit yourself." He lifted the phone to his ear. "Do it."

Cold dread flooded my veins.

"Cruzer won't make it to the finish line."

The voice was low, nearly listless. But the words shot ice through me.

I took off.

Tyson swore, rushing after me, but I moved quicker. I burst through the showroom doors, through the guards, into the vast, dark space where my father's vehicles were arrayed like trophies. The black Aston Martin waited.

Tyson on my heels. "Jules, wait—"

My fingers closed around the keys.

"Stop her!" Victor Montclair's voice boomed behind us.

Tyson scrambled up onto the hood, assuming I wouldn't dare.

He was mistaken.

The tires screeched as I floored it.

He had less than three seconds to jump before I sent the car careening forward, through the half-open garage doors and into the darkness.

The city rushed past me. Adrenaline coursed through my veins.

I had one thought. One prayer.

Please, I want to be on time.

For if I were not, Romy was already dead.

xoxoxo

CHAPTER 16: THE WRECK

Romeo "Romy" Cruzer

The starter girl had her arms raised. I popped the engine. Steady hands.

This was it. Last race. Last chance at something more.

The prize money was everything. It would set us free—me and Jules, free from the Montclairs, free from a life that already had its own ending in blood. I didn't believe in fairy tales, but perhaps I could buy us an escape. A place where her last name wasn't a cage and mine wasn't a death sentence. Somewhere distant, where no one cared who we were.

The flag fell.

And I floored it into the darkness.

The race track was merciless—tightly curved turns, blind spots, strips of asphalt hanging together by a thread. The type of race where you had either nerves of steel or a death wish. The other drivers possessed both.

Six of us.

All ruthless, desperate.

To my right, a red-body Mustang GT with a custom hood scoop. The driver of that one, Zane, was twitchy as all get out, a man who thrived on mayhem. He already was racing for the lead, tires screeching as he cut closer, attempting to squeeze me out.

Behind us, Rico's ride, an Audi R8 with blackout tints and dark blue LED lights. He wasn't just here for the money. He was here for the fame. A street brawler with a god complex, the kind of guy who'd rather crash than lose.

To my left, a Camaro SS, its exhaust smoking fire.

No idea who was driving, but they were hard, cutting lanes like they didn't have anything to lose. Perhaps they didn't.

In front of us, the actual threats.

A Skyline modified, matte black with one white stripe, cutting through the night like a knife. Ava's vehicle. She didn't compete for cash—she competed for sport. A shark in open water. If you were in her path, you were already dead.

And then there was Dez.

He owned a Charger Hellcat, a beast of a vehicle designed for speed and aggression. Dez had been playing longer than the rest of us, and he had one rule—win at all costs. If that meant taking someone off the road, so be it. If that meant cheating, so be it. He'd won more races than I could keep track of. And if I was going to walk away from this, I needed to beat him.

I pressed harder, the city a blur behind me, adrenaline coursing like gasoline through my system. The rumble of engines in my ears.

I was in charge.

Until I wasn't.

The piercing whine of motorcycles sliced through

the rumble of engines, harsh and out of place. It didn't fit here. Not in the race, not on these roads. A misplaced sound in the midst of something that was already a mistake.

I saw the movement in my side mirror—two motorcycles cutting through the pack, their riders riding with precision. Too smooth. Too practiced.

Gunmen.

The first shot. Muzzle flash. A brilliant burst against the black.

The bullet shattered my side-view mirror, showering glass across the dash. I jerked but didn't release the gas. Another shot. This one clipped my front tire. They weren't trying to frighten me.

They were trying to end me.

I swerved, barely dodging another round. Behind me, chaos erupted. A racer panicked, cutting hard into another car's path. Metal shrieked as they collided, one spinning out into the guardrail, the other flipping end over end. Flames burst into the night, the fireball lighting up the track like a warning.

The race wasn't a race anymore.

It was a goddamn execution.

I downshifted, slamming my car into the next turn at a speed that should have been impossible to overcome. My tires wailed, but I managed to maintain control, clinging to the inside lane as a gunman bore down.

He fired. The bullet slammed through my passenger-side window, a clean circle in the glass.

Up ahead, another driver attempted to exploit the confusion, flooring their Skyline to pass me. Mistake.

The shooters weren't after them, but they didn't mind collateral damage. One of the bikers skidded and shot—two, three rounds. The back tire of the Skyline blew up. The driver lost his grip, his car fishtailing before it crashed into the divider. The force sent him flying. The crunch of metal into asphalt made my gut drop, but I didn't glance.

I couldn't.

One of the motorbikes pulled up beside me. Close enough for me to catch the sheen of his gun. He raised it toward my wheel.

I didn't think. I reacted.

I jerked the wheel, striking his front tire.

For a moment, he struggled to regain it. His arms

tightened, his frame contorting around the bike. But it was too late. The motorcycle whirled out of control, the rider catapulting off as his bike crashed, spinning over another racer's course.

Another crash. Another boom.

I breathed out hard through my teeth, white-knuckling the wheel. I could hear sirens now—far off, too distant to make any difference.

More bikers bailed.

I swerved across lanes, attempting to lose them, but they remained fixed on me. My vehicle wasn't designed for this—not for evading bullets, not for escaping alive. The upcoming turn was approaching quickly. If I didn't act now, I'd never have the opportunity.

Then, I spotted it.

A black, sleek Aston Martin slicing through the track, cutting through the mayhem as if it were meant to be here. As if it always had been here.

But I knew better.

Montclair.

Jules.

My gut twisted. She wasn't meant to be here.

And then she was crashing into one of the motorcycles, and the rider flew. Her vehicle moved like a predator, controlled anarchy, steel and velocity with a vengeance.

She came for me.

Gunfire cracked through the air. The remaining racers had either crashed, died, or decided their lives weren't worth the payout. It was just me, Jules, and the gunmen now.

Jules swerved hard, cutting into my lane to shield my car. The roar of her engine filled my ears, drowning out the chaos, the screaming metal, the thunder of bullets.

A shot rang out.

Glass exploded from her rear windshield.

"Jules!"

I grasped the dash, fingers trembling as I flipped to the emergency channel on my Bluetooth. The system hissed, then clicked in.

"Pick up, Montclair. Pick up."

Silence.

I swallowed hard. She could hear me. But she couldn't respond.

My hands gripped the wheel. "Jules, listen to me." My voice sounded rough, shaking with something I wasn't yet willing to call it. "You need to get out of here."

Nothing.

Another bullet whizzed by, missing her driver's side mirror by a hair.

"Goddamn it, Jules! Move it!"

Her taillights flashed like she dithered.

I breathed through my teeth. "I love you."

Nothing.

I had never said it before. Not like that. Not when I knew what it meant.

"I'll love you till I die."

I would die for her.

I was going to die for her.

I revved my engine, ready to make my move— ready to take the hit for her.

And then I saw it.

Jules' car skidded. But not aside.

Directly at the remaining two shooters.

"No—no, no, no!"

The Aston Martin hit the first motorcycle with a

crunch, squashing it beneath the wheels. The rider sailed through the air, slamming onto the pavement with a grotesque crunch. The second shooter attempted to evade, but Jules yanked the wheel at the last moment, her car taking his front tire and spinning him into the guardrail.

The shooting ceased.

But she did too.

Her car went spinning, metal screaming, glass breaking. She crashed into the side barrier with a jarring impact.

And then—nothing.

The sort of nothing that could only signal one thing.

No.

I yanked the wheel, barely registering the tires screaming under my control.

She wasn't moving.

The last gunman—the one Jules hadn't injured—staggered to his feet, blood running down his face. Gun still clutched in his hand.

He raised it.

Jules was conscious now, attempting to move. To

get out.

She wouldn't make it in time.

I didn't think. I reacted.

I put my car into a hard spin, skidding between her and the shooter.

The muzzle flared.

A searing pain burst in my side.

I heard the shot before I felt the bullet rip through me.

Jules was yelling my name.

She was reversing, trying to reach me.

I slumped against the wheel.

The world spun, tilting on its side. Smoke. Blood. Squealing tires.

Then nothing.

I surfaced through the dark, my body weightless, like I was floating between worlds. There was a ringing in my ears, distant voices slipping in and out of focus, too far away to hold on to. My fingers twitched, but they felt disconnected from me, like they belonged to someone else.

I tried to breathe. My ribs ached. My throat burned.

Then—too bright lights. Too clean air. The sterile scent of antiseptic curling at the edges of my awareness.

I did not wake up in my bedroom.

Because the sheets were too clean. Bleached. Too stiff, as if they'd been washed raw. As if they didn't fit me. As if I didn't fit into them.

The moment I tried to shift, agony hit me—blinding and fierce, burning through my ribs like a knife. My side seared. My head pounded, a slow, relentless drumming in sync with the beep of the machine on the bedside table.

I took a breath. It struggled past my lungs.

"Jules."

Her name was a blessing and a curse, a knife turning deeper with each passing second she wasn't around.

I attempted to sit up. My body refused to play along.

Snapshots assaulted me in fractured fragments—metal crunching, glass shattering, the crunch of her car colliding with the barrier. The blood. The silence.

No. No.

Footsteps. A door creaking open.

I shifted my head.

Uncle Rafa blocked the doorway, arms folded. Marco standing next to him, fists jammed into his pockets. Their faces were sculpted from stone, impossible to read.

Something was wrong.

"She's gone."

The words struck me like a bullet.

I swallowed, my parched throat. "Where is she?"

Rafa didn't respond immediately. Just breathed out, slow and deep. Measured. Marco's gaze broke away.

That was all it took.

I knew.

Something within me snapped wide open, like the windshield I'd seen her smash through.

"No," I said, shaking my head. Hurting to move. Hurting to breathe. "No, she—"

Rafa didn't glance at me.

"She's gone," he said again.

But I wasn't dumb. I knew what people meant when they didn't want to say the truth aloud.

Marco shifted his weight. Cleared his throat. "Romy—"

I didn't catch the rest.

Because I was already drowning.

My monitor next to me beeped faster. The room blurred, fluorescent lights too intense, white walls closing in on me. I hauled myself up, trying to ignore the burn in my ribs, the way my body felt like it would buckle beneath its own weight.

"I have to see her." The words hardly made it out of my mouth.

Rafa finally regarded me. A flash of something in his eyes—pity.

That was it. That was enough.

The wreckage engulfed me completely.

And this time, I allowed it.

×o×o×o

CHAPTER 17: TWO FAMILIES

Montclair and Cruzer

"Two families, unalike in reputation and ruthlessness,
In the heart of Toronto, where our story unfolds,
From a new vendetta, new violence ignites,
And the streets run red with sins unatoned.
Born from the fury of these warring clans,
A pair of lovers defy their fate;
But their doomed love, marked by tragedy,
Is the only thing that can end the hate.
The path of their love, shadowed by death,
And the fury of fathers that time won't quell,
Only in the silence of their children's fall,
Does the war between them finally mend."

Victor Montclair's phone rang before he even had a chance to take a breath. The scent of leather and motor oil lingered in the air, a constant presence in his showroom office. He barely glanced at the caller ID before answering, his expression unreadable. The words on the other end—hospital, emergency, critical condition—hit him like a cold blade. He didn't need to ask questions. Didn't need to process. He was already moving, shoving his chair back and grabbing his coat, his mind racing faster than his body as he strode toward the exit.

"Tyson, move the car," Victor snapped, shoving his phone into his pocket.

Tyson Vega, his right-hand man, his nephew, didn't ask questions. He was already dashing for the black Range Rover parked out front. The city whizzed by as they rushed to St. Joseph's Hospital, dodging cars, cutting corners like it mattered.

Victor did not pray. He did not beg. He had learned years ago that the world did not hear men like him. But as he balled his fists, he felt something akin to fear creeping in.

Across town, the phone rang at the Cruzer Auto & Body.

Raul Cruzer picked it up, his tone crisp, as if he already knew bad news was on the line.

"What?"

A few seconds of silence, then his knuckles whitened around the receiver. "We're coming." He hung up without another word.

Gabi Cruzer saw the look in her husband's eyes before he could hide it. "Raul—"

"Get in the car."

She didn't ask. Didn't push. Just nodded and grabbed her coat.

Marcus "Marco" Cruzer and Tino Delgado were already outside when Raul emerged onto the porch. Marco was revving his bike, sitting on it, while Tino stood against the hood of a matte-black Charger, concern etched across his face.

"What happened?" Marco asked, dropping the cigarette from his hand.

"Hospital," Raul said, his voice strained. "Now."

No questions. No pause. Just action.

The emergency room hallway was a battlefield.

No guns, no knives, no blood spilled—so far. Just two families on opposite sides of a battlefield, caught in a silence that weighed more heavily than fists.

The Montclairs were on one side. Victor Montclair at the front, his face chipped out of stone, Tyson Vega at his side, arms folded, shoulders set. Their very presence dominated the space, a wordless warning to anyone who dared to breathe too loudly.

The Cruzers, on the other hand. Raul's jaw clenched so hard his teeth seemed ready to crack, Marco's fingers quivering at his sides like he needed something to grasp—something to shatter. Tino was at his side, attempting to play the mediator, but even he seemed seconds from losing it. Uncle Rafa, though, was beyond that.

The tension between them hung in the air like something unseen, something heavier than the flashing neon lights beyond the walls. Blood debts. Bodies buried where no one should ever dig. Oaths taken in whispers and betrayed in bullet fire.

It should have been about their war. Their scores. Their own rules.

Tonight, all that was irrelevant.

Tonight, their children were dying to live.

The emergency room was a whirl of motion—masked nurses with their faces low, doctors yelling orders, stretchers whizzing by, wheels scraping on linoleum. The fluorescent lights hummed, bright and sterile. The tile was splattered with footprints, some damp from the rain outside, some dry with some darker substance. The entire facility smelled of antiseptic and terror.

And then Uncle Rafa spoke.

His voice was low, but every word was carved from glass. Sharp. Ready to cut.

"This is on you, Montclair." His fists curled at his sides, knuckles bloodstained. "I should put a bullet in your head right now."

Victor Montclair didn't flinch. He had been through worse. But even he couldn't hide the tension in his shoulders, the slight twitch in his jaw. "Watch your mouth, Cruzer. You're standing in a hospital, not a back alley."

"If my nephew dies—" Rafa took a step forward, but Marco caught his arm, holding him back. "—I swear to God, I'll—"

"Enough."

The voice cut through the room like a blade.

Detective Harris.

His badge glinted in the bright lights, his feet planted firmly between both families. The only thing preventing this hallway from becoming a crime scene.

"You think I don't see what this is?" Harris's voice was rasp, weary. "Two kids bleeding out because neither of you two could get along."

Victor's gaze grew dark. "If you're implying—"

"I'm not implying anything damn thing." Harris interrupted him, tone low, deadly. "I'm telling you. If either one of them dies tonight, this city burns."

There was a silence then.

The only thing to hear was the slow beep of equipment beyond the doors, the faint shout of doctors calling out instructions. The kind of sound you don't catch unless you're waiting for something you can't influence.

Tyson Vega moved forward, his eyes focusing on Uncle Rafa like a sniper on target.

"Perhaps you should have kept your nephew under control rather than allowing him to brainwash

Juliet into this disaster," he said, his voice cutting like a razor. "She was never supposed to be with him.

Marco snorted, his head shaking. Yeah? And what was she supposed to be, huh? Locked in your little tower? Dressed up like a Montclair princess while you planned out what—a marriage to one of your goons?"

Tyson's fists curled. "At least we don't let our own get killed on the streets like animals."

The air became thick enough to choke.

Then, the emergency room doors burst open.

A physician stepped in, his blue scrubs bespattered with dark spots. His mask was down, sweat beading his brow. He looked tired. Emptied out.

Both families froze.

"We need a report," Victor spoke first, his voice tense, but just.

The physician took a breath, scanning them. "We're doing all we can. But they both are critical."

Silence.

He put a hand through his hair, the movement slow, calculated—like he understood that whatever came out of his mouth next would alter everything.

"Juliet Montclair had a subdural hematoma—

bleeding in her head. We did an emergency craniotomy to decompress, but she's still not responding. Her body's in shock, her vitals unstable." His eyes darted across the hallway. "Romeo Cruzer had several internal injuries—ruptured spleen, collapsed lung, two broken ribs pressing uncomfortably close to his heart. We did what we could, but he lost a great deal of blood. Too much."

Marco drew a slow breath. "What are you saying?"

The doctor's face was somber. "I'm saying that if they get through the night, it'll be a miracle."

There was a silence that weighed more than before between them.

Victor Montclair blew out a breath, rubbing his hand across his face. Uncle Rafa's gaze was fixed on the bloodstains drying on his knuckles. Marco swallowed hard, jaw clenching so tightly his teeth would shatter.

Harris crossed his arms. "You both understand how this works. If one of them dies, there's no holding back what happens next. So we do it now. Here."

Victor Montclair's eyes darted toward the doors, toward whatever room Juliet was in. And for the first time that night, something in him broke.

"What sort of deal are we making?" he asked, voice low, but with something sharp-edged.

Uncle Rafa sucked in a sharp breath. "No more bloodshed. No more hunting one another down. Whatever becomes of those kids inside, we put an end to this tonight."

Harris nodded. "That is, no retaliation, no backroom deals, no clandestine payback at night. You all leave. You allow them to choose how this finishes."

For an interminable moment, nobody said anything.

Then Victor patted his coat pocket, pulled out a cigar, rolled it in his fingers, and put it back in position. A leisurely sigh, a look down at the floor.

"Fine," he said. "It's settled then."

Uncle Rafa clenched his teeth, but nodded.

The war was on pause. But everyone in that hallway knew what was really going on.

If Romeo Cruzer and Juliet Montclair didn't make it out alive, there would be no deal in the world that could stop what came next.

xoxoxo

CHAPTER 18: THE ROAD AHEAD

Juliet "Jules" Montclair

Adrenaline had a metallic flavor. Cutting. Scorching.

It seared through my veins as I stamped on the gas. The Aston Martin growled in reply, a living animal beneath my hands, slicing through the bedlam like a knife.

The night was a battlefront. Bullets ripped the air. Cars screamed. Tires screamed. I hardly felt my own heartbeat under the noise, under the raw speed ripping through my frame.

A motorcycle zipped by my flank. Its driver wheeled around, training his weapon directly at me.

I didn't blink. I didn't think.

I jerked the wheel. My vehicle scraped against his motorcycle, metal on metal. He went flying—his body twisting in mid-air before hitting the pavement. A greasy crunch. A splatter of red.

One down.

But there were others.

The rest had fled—some killed, some determining their lives weren't worth the prize money. But the ones who remained? They weren't here for the money.

They were here to kill Romy.

It was just me, Romy, and them now.

I cut into his lane, blocking his car as I surged ahead. Romy didn't require my assistance—he was a specter behind the wheel, dodging gaps, anticipating movement before it occurred—but I couldn't leave him exposed.

And then the bullet arrived.

A snap through the night.

Glass shattered behind me.

Shards poured down, cutting through the

blackness, snagging in my hair, flashing like shattered stars.

"Jules!"

Romy's voice crackled through the Bluetooth speakers, sharp, frantic.

I attempted to respond, but my throat had shut, my breath knotted somewhere between fear and rebellion.

"Pick up, Montclair. Pick up."

Silence.

But I heard it in his breathing—the panic he never allowed to escape.

"Jules, listen to me." His voice was rough, laced with something I did not wish to identify. "You need to get the hell out of here, okay?"

I clutched the wheel harder.

"Goddamn it, Jules! Move it!"

I stalled. A fraction of a second. Practically nothing.

Then—

"I love you."

My heart sank.

He'd never said it to me before. Not like that. Not

when it counted. Not when we both knew it was something permanent.

"I'll love you till I die."

And the thing about Romy was that he didn't make empty promises.

I wished I could tell him the same thing.

Wanted to let the words rip through my throat, raw and real and wild. But I didn't.

Because only one of us was getting out of this track alive.

And it wasn't going to be me.

I took a ragged breath, vision narrowing. The world dwindled to one point.

And I made my decision.

I shifted gears, tires shrieking, and punched my car ahead—right into the last two shooters.

"Jules—NO—"

Romy's voice was far away. An echo I no longer heard.

The first motorcycle buckled under my tires, the rider tossed like a rag doll into the darkness. The second attempted to make a turn, but I jerked the wheel, cutting off his tire. He spun out and crashed into the guardrail.

The gunfire stopped.

But so did I.

The Aston Martin swirled out, metal screaming, glass shattering. My body was shoved forward, seatbelt cutting deep as the car smashed into the barrier.

And then—

Nothing.

A silence so heavy it was like drowning.

I attempted to move. My fingers clawed at the door handle, feeble and trembling.

I had to escape.

Had to—

A shadow lurched out.

The final gunman.

Blood trickled down his face, his arm limp, broken. But his gun was still clutched in his hand.

He brought it up.

Pointed it at me.

I knew, in that instant, I wouldn't make it in time.

And neither would Romy.

But Romy didn't think.

He acted.

His car swooped between us.

A steel barrier slamming into place.

The gun fired.

One shot.

Romy jerked.

His body crumpled against the wheel. Fingers relaxing.

No.

NO.

"Romy!"

My vehicle lurched as I backed up, tires squealing, spinning.

He was leaning forward. Head cocked. Blood spreading on his side.

The world went fuzzy.

Gunfire.

Smoke.

Screaming tires.

And then—

Blackness.

Consciousness was a fickle thing. It eluded my grasp like grains of sand, taunting me with glimpses of light and sound before pulling me under once more.

The first time I surfaced, the world was all too bright. White, sanitary walls. The beeping hum of a machine somewhere nearby. My body ripped asunder and sewn together with flame.

I moved my head—torturously slow.

And there he was.

Romy.

He was in the bed beside me, chest rising and falling in a slow, fragile rhythm. Bruises spread across his skin, stark against the sheets. His arm was wrapped, his side bound in gauze. Alive, but just barely.

I wanted to touch him. Wanted to call his name. But the pull of unconsciousness was dragging me back down, unrelenting.

Another fall into the dark.

Another stolen moment.

When I opened my eyes again, the room felt different. Blurred faces. Muted voices.

The doors of the emergency bay opened, and for one, broken moment, I saw him.

Victor Montclair.

My father.

And he wasn't alone.

The Cruzers.

They were there, talking in hushed tones. Measured. Calculated. And then—

A handshake.

A bargain.

What were they shaking hands over?

I struggled to keep hold of the idea, to rationalize the image burning itself into my mind. But again, the blackness swept in on me, quicker this time.

The monitors hooked up around me beeped warning.

And then—nothing.

I awoke to white walls and the antiseptic smell of hospital.

Pain pulsed through me, a slow, pitiless hurt sewn into my bones. My body was weak, my limbs alien, but none of it counted. None of it even registered because—

Romy.

The mere idea of him dying was a bullet to the chest. My heart skipped a beat. I sat up too quickly, the motion shooting knives through my ribs.

"Easy," a voice cautioned.

My head jerked toward it.

Victor Montclair.

My father.

He stood at my bedside, stance perfect, face impassive. But I was not fooled. Knew how to see beyond the gleaming facade.

His fists were knotted at his sides. A giveaway.

I swallowed hard as my throat caught fire. "Where is he?"

There was a hesitation.

Then my father sat down in the chair next to my bed, moving slowly, methodically. Careful in a manner I had never witnessed before.

"I thought I was going to lose you."

I looked away, at the IV in my arm, at the bruises that colored my skin.

"You almost did."

There was silence between us. Not cold. Just. present.

Then he let out a breath, running a hand over his face. "I don't want to fight anymore."

I gave a harsh, humorless laugh. "Since when?"

He didn't respond right away. When he did, his

voice was gentler than I had ever heard it.

"Because I sat in this room and understood there was a version of my life where you never woke up."

I drew in a slow, trembling breath.

He reached out—hesitated—then placed his hand over mine. His hold was firm, anchoring, but gentle, as if he was afraid I'd disappear if he held on too hard.

"I know I can't change everything overnight, but I need you to understand, Juliet—I am sorry for everything."

The truth hung between us, delicate and true.

I didn't know if I had forgiven him.

Didn't know if I ever would.

But perhaps—perhaps this was all that was needed for now.

I breathed out.

And clamped his hand back.

There was a moment. Then another. The quiet was heavy, bearing down on my head.

I pushed my voice through the lump in my throat. "Where is Romy?"

My father went rigid.

"Where is he?" I asked again, heaving myself into

a sitting position despite the protest of my body.

Victor's eyes flashed away for the slightest moment. A hesitation.

And then he said it.

"He's gone."

The world spun.

Gone.

Not here. Not waiting for me.

Dead.

The word was not said, but I heard it just the same. Felt it like a knife sliced between my ribs.

"No." My voice broke, shattering in my throat. "No, you're lying."

Victor didn't protest. Didn't temper the blow with words of comfort. Merely sat there with something strangely akin to pity in his eyes.

The breath in my chest turned to ice.

A cry escaped my lips—something raw, something shattered. My hands grasped at the sheets, at the IV in my arm, at anything that would ground me to a world that felt suddenly too much to bear.

I had seen him in that bed. I had seen him breathing. Hadn't I?

I clamped my hands to my face as the first cry ripped through me. Then another. And another.

My body shook, wracked with grief so heavy it felt like drowning.

My father said nothing. Did not attempt to console me.

Because he knew.

Nothing he could ever say would bring Romy back.

XoXoXo

CHAPTER 19: BREAKOUT

Romeo "Romy" Cruzer

Pain is a slow-burning thing.

It doesn't hit all at once—not the way bullets do, not the way a car spins out on slick asphalt. It creeps in, latching onto your bones, sitting heavy in your chest, whispering in your ear when the world is too damn quiet.

I felt it every morning when I woke up—muscles stiff, ribs aching. Felt it in the way my knee locked up when I stood too fast, in the way my fingers twitched when I reached for my phone—only to stop, because there was no one left to call.

Jules was gone.

And I was still here.

My family took me back in like I was some fragile thing, like I hadn't spent my whole life dodging worse. My mom hovered—bringing tea I didn't drink, soup I didn't touch, blankets I never asked for. My dad, never one for softness, just patted my shoulder when he passed by, which was his way of saying, *I'm glad you made it, kid.*

But I wasn't.

My father wasn't the type to say much. His love came in unspoken rules and expectations, the weight of his presence enough to remind me that I owed him. That I owed *this*—this life I still had—to something bigger than luck.

But my mother tried. She was always trying, always believing that if she just reached far enough, she could pull me back from whatever edge I was teetering on. But I was tired of being pulled. Tired of being treated like something that needed saving.

Marco showed up at the garage on a Wednesday, like he hadn't been avoiding me since that night.

For a long second, he just stood there, hands in his jacket pockets, scanning me like I was some wreckage he wasn't sure could be salvaged. Then he exhaled sharply and shook his head.

"You look like shit."

"Yeah, well." I wiped my hands on a rag, not bothering to look up. "Life's been a real party."

Marco let out a dry laugh, but it faded too fast. "I didn't mean for things to go down like that."

I didn't either.

The last time we talked, we were throwing punches. But that night didn't matter anymore. None of it did.

I sighed, tossing the rag onto the workbench. "Yeah. Me neither."

Marco grinned, and just like that, it was done.

Tino didn't treat me like I was made of glass.

While everyone else tiptoed around me, he handed me a wrench and told me to get my shit together.

We worked in silence most days, the sound of metal and oil filling the spaces where words should've been. But every now and then, he'd break it—always in that same calm, matter-of-fact way of his.

"She wouldn't want this, you know."

I stiffened.

He didn't say her name, but he didn't have to.

"She's gone, Tino." My voice came out rougher than I meant.

His gaze didn't waver. "And you're still acting like you are."

I had nothing to say to that.

Because he wasn't wrong.

But the truth didn't change anything.

Jules was dead.

And I was still here.

I should've looked it up sooner.

I don't know why I didn't. Maybe some part of me thought that if I didn't see it, it wouldn't be real.

But pretending only lasted so long.

When I finally pulled out my phone and searched her name, there was nothing. No obituary. No funeral announcements. No pictures.

Nothing.

I frowned, scrolled, searched again.

Still nothing.

But there *was* a news report—some half-assed

story about "malfunctioning vehicles" at an illegal street race. Multiple casualties. Multiple dead.

No names. No faces. No truth.

There was nothing on Jules.

Looked like the Montclairs had done a damn good job burying the story.

And Detective Harris? He'd swept it under the rug, same as always.

I should've been angry. I *was* angry. But more than that? I was tired. Tired of living in a city that erased the things that mattered. Tired of chasing ghosts.

Tired of waiting for a girl who was never coming back.

Dinner with my family was the same as it always was—loud, messy, plates being passed like we weren't a family full of criminals and street racers who made our living cutting deals in the back alleys of Toronto. The table smelled like home—garlic, slow-roasted meat, the faint trace of motor oil clinging to my dad's hands even though he'd scrubbed them clean.

But something about tonight felt different.

Maybe it was me.

I wasn't sure when I made the decision, but by the

time my mom set a plate in front of me, I knew. The words sat on my tongue, heavy like lead.

I set down my fork. Cleared my throat.

"I'm finishing school."

Silence.

For the first time in my life, my family had nothing to say.

"You—" My mom blinked, like she hadn't heard me right. "You're what?"

I exhaled through my nose, shifting my weight. "I have one year left. Might as well get my diploma."

A beat. Then—

My dad nodded. Just once. "Good."

That was it. No arguments, no sarcastic remarks. Just one word, weighted with more meaning than I was ready for.

Maybe they saw it too—the way something in me had shifted, the way I wasn't the same Romy who had spent his nights burning rubber and outrunning the cops for fun. Maybe almost dying did that to a person. Maybe losing Jules did.

Uncle Rafa cleared his throat, reaching for his glass of whiskey. His hair was more gray than black now, and the lines on his face had deepened, but the sharp edge in his eyes was still there. Just softened.

"School's a good call, mijo," he said, swirling the glass in his hand. "You got too much of your mama in you to rot in this life forever."

I huffed a laugh. "Don't let Dad hear you say that."

Rafa smirked. "He knows. That's why he doesn't fight you on it." He took a slow sip, eyes locking onto mine. "Listen, kid. I spent my whole damn life thinking I had to play the hand I was dealt. That this was all there was." He gestured vaguely to the house, to the garage, to the world we were all tangled up in. "And I was wrong."

I frowned. "You regretting something?"

His mouth pulled into something almost like a smile, but it didn't quite reach his eyes.

"Just saying," he murmured, tapping a finger against the side of his glass. "You still got a choice. Before this life sinks its teeth into you for good."

I didn't say anything. Because I wasn't sure I believed him.

But finishing school was only the first step.

Because Toronto wasn't my home anymore.

It was a graveyard.

Every street, every alley, every intersection—I could still see her there. Jules, leaning against the hood of my car, a smirk twisting at the edges of her mouth. Jules, tossing me a cigarette she knew I wouldn't smoke, just to piss me off. Jules, standing in the middle of the road, headlights bleeding into the night behind her, saying, *catch me if you can.*

And I did. Every damn time.

Except the last.

So I used my old contacts, wiped the slate clean. Sold my car. Scrubbed my name from the streets.

Romy Cruzer had vanished from the racing scene without a trace.

Didn't matter. My last name still carried weight, still got whispers in garages and hushed conversations behind neon-lit storefronts.

But I wasn't looking for trouble anymore.

Some nights, I lay awake, staring at the ceiling, wondering if Jules would've hated me for it.

If she would've called me a coward.

If she would've whispered my name in the dark

the way I whispered hers, a prayer, a curse, a wound that refused to heal.

I pictured her hands—calloused fingertips, chipped nail polish, the faint scar on her knuckle from the time she broke a guy's nose for touching her without asking.

I imagined them curling into fists, shoving me against the hood of my car, voice sharp and wild, telling me, *this isn't who you are.*

But she was gone.

And I was still here.

For now.

XoXoXo

CHAPTER 20: SACRIFICE

Juliet "Jules" Montclair

The first thing I remembered waking up to was the antiseptic smell and the beat of a heart monitor. A steady, rhythmic beep. Like a metronome. Like a countdown.

The second thing I remembered was pain.

Not the stabbing kind—not the kind of thing that happens in movies, or in books. Just this dull, throbbing ache in my head, as if someone had opened me up and scooped out the inside of my skull. Which, I suppose, they had.

The surgeons told me the operation had been successful. That I was fortunate. That swelling had subsided, and my brain activity remained intact.

But I didn't feel fortunate.

Because sometimes, I would blink and miss out on whole minutes.

Sometimes, I would grasp for a memory—a trivial one, something as mundane as the way I drank my coffee or the name of the nurse who took my vital signs—and find nothing.

Sometimes, I'd close my eyes and see headlights. Metal twisting. The rush of impact.

And sometimes, I'd see him.

Romy, his face half-lit by the glow of the dashboard. Romy, smirking at me from across the street, an unlit cigarette dangling from his lips. Romy, whispering my name like it was something sacred, something stolen.

I recalled his car, the warmth of the engine still vibrating under my legs as I leaned back, panting, fingers bunched into his shirt. The air was heavy, heavy with gasoline and something sweeter—us, wrapped up in leather seats and poor choices.

"Jules," he had whispered against my skin, voice raw, ruined.

I had pulled my fingers through his hair, yanking, pulling him closer. His hands were all over—across my waist, under my shirt, pushing into my ribs as if he could hold me in place, keep me from getting away.

"This is a mistake," I had whispered.

"Then stop me."

I hadn't.

Because with Romy, it had never been about reason.

It was about the way his mouth rammed against mine, hungry and insistent. The way his body surrounded me, the smell of motor oil and sweat combining with something darker, something perilously close to love.

It was about the way he moaned when I nipped at his lip, the way his hands shook when he reached out to touch me, as if he knew this would be the downfall of us but still couldn't resist.

It was about the fire. The anger. The unescapable draw of him.

I remembered it all.

But I didn't know if anything of it had been real.

I spent weeks struggling to become stronger.

Physical therapy was slow, painful. Each step a betrayal—my body fighting to recall how to perform something it had done a million times. My muscles had become strangers, and my bones hurt as if they were rejecting me entirely. I despised the helplessness, the way my limbs trembled from the slightest movement. I despised the sterile walls, the artificial glow of the rehabilitation center, the overly cheerful encouragement of the therapists.

I loathed the way people gazed at me these days— as if I were breakable, as if I were something to be shielded.

I wasn't.

I had never been.

But the hardest thing wasn't the pain. Or the PT. Or the fact that my own face was strange to me, that I was staring at a ghost.

The hardest thing was the quiet.

No Romy.

No word. No mention. No obit, no accident notice. As if he'd never lived.

At first, I told myself it was the memory lapses. That perhaps I was forgetting something important, something that everyone else already knew. But late at night, when the world slowed down and my body hurt too much to sleep, I picked up my phone and searched.

Romeo Cruzer.

Nothing.

No wreckage. No street race gone horribly wrong. No obituary.

I searched the web, delving into chat rooms, following street racing bulletin boards, sifting through all the backchannels I could remember. But it was like pursuing smoke—each lead fizzled out into static, each post that had ever mentioned him was erased. Scrubbed.

As if someone had erased him from the map.

And I knew who could do that.

The first time I inquired, my dad did not even glance at me. He simply folded the newspaper he was faking to read and breathed slowly, as if he had been anticipating this moment.

The second time, I did not let him dismiss me.

"Did you do it?" I asked one night, sitting there as

he poured whiskey into a glass. His movements were slow, calculated, as if he was weighing every last drop before it splashed into the crystal.

He seemed older now. Softer, even. As if he'd finally laid down the burden of whatever war he'd been waging all these years.

He rotated the glass in his hand, observing the amber liquid spin before he took a calculated sip. "No," he said.

I wished to believe him.

Perhaps I did.

But it didn't alter the reality that Romy was gone.

And I remained here.

Somewhere along the ruins of recovery, something between us shifted.

It wasn't overnight. It wasn't some epiphanic realization or tearful apology. But small things began to change.

It was silence initially—the sort that wasn't awkward, but. simpler. The way he ceased reminding me of Montclair & Motors. The way he came to my sessions in silence, sitting in the therapy room's corner while I strained through the ache. The way his hand remained an inch from my back when we were out and about, as though he wanted to steady me but was smart enough to keep trying.

Then came the conversations. Small ones, at first. A question about how I was feeling. A comment about the hospital food being absolute garbage. A joke about how I still drove better than Tyson Vega, even after brain surgery.

I let them happen.

One day, he handed me an envelope without saying a word. I opened it with trembling fingers, expecting another burden, another expectation wrapped in expensive letterhead.

Instead, it was an acceptance letter. France. Engineering.

I read it twice, then looked up at my father.

"I didn't apply."

"I did."

The words landed like a slap.

I let out a slow breath, gripping the letter between my fingers. "You can't just decide my future for me."

His expression didn't change. "I didn't decide. I gave you an option."

I huffed out a humorless laugh. "An option you forged my name for?"

He didn't answer.

I looked back down at the letter, its heaviness in my palms. College. The term seemed far away, something from another life I was no longer a part of. Something that had been intended for the girl prior to the accident. Prior to the scars. Prior to Romy.

I hadn't submitted a single application. Hadn't even considered it.

"Juliet." My father's voice was quieter now, the edge worn down. "You need to decide soon."

I swallowed, still staring at the paper in my hands.

"I'll think about it."

His nod was small, almost imperceptible. He didn't push, and that was new. The old him would've demanded an answer. Laid out the path he'd already chosen for me.

Maybe something had shifted between us.

Or perhaps he was only waiting for me to get it right.

If I even had any idea.

Dominic Langford appeared on a Sunday.

I was out, looking at the skyline, trying to pretend the aching in my head wasn't making the world spin. The pain had turned into something persistent now— not needle-sharp, not excruciating, just present. A constant reminder that I was no longer the same girl who had once kissed Romy with greasy hands in the back of his car. That girl had died on a race track, months ago.

Dominic moved cautiously—too cautiously. As if he feared I'd break if he moved closer.

"Jules."

I faced him, drinking in the crisp suit, the high-end watch, the way his fingers curled inward at his sides, as if he was coiling for a blow.

He wore the same expression everyone wore for me now—thinly disguised concern, as if I were some breakable, broken thing. It was draining.

"How are you?" he asked.

I didn't respond.

I didn't know how.

Fine wasn't true. Neither was not fine. It wasn't even that I didn't have words—it was that I didn't know which ones were mine anymore. So I just breathed in slow and glanced over at the sky.

"You don't have to tell me," I said instead.

He paused. "Tell you what?"

"That this isn't going to work."

A beat.

Then, to my surprise, he let out a soft, almost relieved laugh.

"No," he confessed. "I guess I don't."

We sat quietly for a time, the expectation piling up between us, thread by thread. It was curious, how simple it felt to shed it—it was like a cumbersome coat I'd worn for so long that I'd lost track of the fact that I could shed it.

Eventually, he looked at me. "I hope you find all that you desire."

His voice was quieter than I'd ever known it.

I looked at him, the fringes of him fading a bit from the headache throbbing at the back of my eyes. "I hope you do too."

And there it was.

No big words. No sobbing. Only the soft slam of a door that had never really been open to begin with.

I should have felt free.

But freedom wasn't the same without Romy.

My father did not object when I told him that I was not going to be heir to Montclair & Motors.

The old him would have. Would have contested this with me, would have spoken of how this is who we are, our legacy.

Now, though, he simply nodded.

"I know," he stated simply.

And when I explained I was going to France—taking my spot at the high-level engineering program, creating something that was mine—he smiled.

Not a smile of business. Not politics.

A genuine one.

"You're more than just a Montclair," he said, voice calm. "You always have been."

Something in my chest had cracked open.

I didn't thank him. He wasn't expecting me to.

But for the first time, I saw him as he was. Not a villain. Not a dark figure in my life.

Just a father. Doing his best.

And right now, that was enough.

I exhaled, shifting my stance. "Tyson would make a better successor than me," I said, watching his expression carefully. "He's built for this—he wants it. He understands the business, the industry, the people. He *wants* Montclair & Motors to be his future. I never did."

My father studied me for a long moment, then nodded again, slow and measured. "I know."

It wasn't a concession. It wasn't defeat. It was understanding.

"I'm proud of you," he said.

For the first time, I trusted him.

I departed from Toronto with a battered heart full of peace

No goodbyes. No looking back.

But as the plane soared, I leaned my forehead against the glass and breathed his name softly.

A prayer.

A curse.

A hurt that would not mend.

Because Romy was no more.

And I was still here.

For now.

XoXoXo

CHAPTER 21: STAR-CROSSED SORROW

Romeo "Romy" Cruzer

A year later, Toronto still smelled the same—hot asphalt and cold consequence.

I rolled through the city with the windows down, letting the air sting my skin, letting the skyline carve itself into my bones like it never left. Like I never left. But I had. And I wasn't the same reckless kid gunning for an escape.

This time, I was here on my own terms.

Cruzer Auto & Body looked smaller than I

remembered. The metal shutters were half-down, like my uncle couldn't decide if the shop was open for business or closed for good. I knew that feeling too well.

I killed the ignition and stepped out. The pavement crackled under my boots as I walked toward the place that raised me, the place that nearly buried me. Inside, the air smelled like burnt oil, cheap coffee, and a past I wasn't sure I could ever shake.

Uncle Rafa was at the counter, arms crossed, gaze heavy as a set of bad odds.

"Didn't think you were coming back," he said, voice rough with smoke and history.

"Yeah, well." I exhaled sharply. "Guess I ran out of places to go."

His eyes flickered over me, reading between the lines, finding the truths I hadn't said. Then he just nodded. No grand speeches, no questions. That was the thing about family—you didn't always need words to know what came next.

I took in the shop, the walls I'd practically grown-up in. The neon-lit garage that had been more of a home than my own house. The weight of the past pressed against my ribs like a phantom fist.

"You clean this place up?" I asked, eyeing the organized shelves, the lack of backdoor business deals lurking in the shadows.

"Someone had to," he said. "Wasn't gonna let your old man's mistakes drown us."

Raul Cruzer. My father. A man who could build anything with his hands but couldn't fix the cracks in his own damn life.

"Where is he?"

Rafa's jaw tensed. "Gone."

"Gone, as in—?"

"As in he walked out one night and never came back." His voice was flat, unreadable. "Gabi finally let him go. Maybe you should too."

I scoffed. Let go? Like it was that easy. Like he hadn't spent my whole life making sure I could never really leave.

The garage door screeched open, and Tino stepped in, wiping grease off his hands. His face lit up when he saw me. "Shit. Look who finally decided to show."

I smirked. "Miss me?"

"Hell no," he shot back, grinning. Then, quieter, "You good?"

I hesitated. "Getting there."

Marco swaggered in next, all wild energy and bad decisions, and clapped a hand on my shoulder. "'Bout damn time, hermano. Thought you were too good for us now."

"Nah." I shook my head. "Just needed to figure some things out."

Marco's gaze sharpened, sensing the shift in me, the way I carried myself differently. He didn't push. Not yet.

"So?" Rafa leaned against the counter, watching me carefully. "You just passing through, or you here for real?"

I looked around the garage—the place I once swore I'd never come back to. The place I was trying to make something real out of.

"I'm here," I said. "For real."

And that's when something slammed against the garage door behind me. Hard.

I jolted, my heart punching against my ribs as a loud cackle echoed through the shop.

The door flew open, and out lunged—

"BOO!"

Raul Cruzer, laughing his ass off, hands on his knees like he'd just won the lottery off my misery.

My father.

Alive.

Not dead in some ditch. Not rotting in a jail cell. Just here. Laughing like this was the funniest thing in the damn world.

I inhaled sharply, my pulse still jackhammering against my throat. "What the hell is wrong with you?"

My Dad wiped at his eyes, still grinning. "What? You think I was gonna let you come back without a proper welcome?"

I ran a hand down my face, half-relieved, half-murderous. "Rafa told me you left."

He snorted. "I did. For like—what? Three weeks?" He glanced at Rafa. "Three weeks, right?"

Rafa didn't even look up. "Felt longer."

"I had some things to clear up," He went on, dragging a chair over and slumping into it. "But you know me, kid. Always find my way home."

"Yeah?" I crossed my arms. "And what exactly did

you clear up?"

His smirk twitched, something darker flickering beneath it. "Business."

Right. Because with Raul Cruzer, business never meant something legal.

Before I could respond, the back-office door opened, and my mother stepped out.

Gabi Cruzer wasn't the type to cry when she saw her son walk through the door. She wasn't soft. Life didn't let her be. But when her eyes landed on me, something in them cracked.

"You look tired," she said, scanning my face like she was checking for damage.

"Long drive."

"You eat?"

I almost laughed. "Nice to see you too, Ma."

She huffed, but I saw the tension in her shoulders ease. "You staying?"

I nodded. "Yeah. I'm here."

She reached out, fixing my collar like I was still sixteen. Then she gave me a firm nod, like that was the only confirmation she needed.

And then, because Marco was incapable of letting

a moment breathe, he clapped his hands together. "Alright, now that we've established Romy isn't dead—who's hungry?"

Tino snorted. "Did you even work today?"

"I supervised."

"Supervised my ass."

Rafa shook his head, but there was something lighter in his face. A small shift, almost like relief.

And me?

I looked around at all of them—the only people in the world who truly knew me.

The past wasn't something you could outrun. It stayed with you, sunk into your skin like grease and gasoline.

But maybe, just maybe, you could build something new out of it.

For the first time in a long time, I believed that.

The shop smelled different now.

Not in a bad way—just… different.

Before, Cruzer Auto & Body had reeked of illicit deals and backdoor business, of fast cash and even faster exits. But now? Now it smelled like hard work, like oil and sweat and the kind of honest labor I used to laugh at.

I wiped my hands on a rag, stepping back from the '72 Chevelle on the lift. "That should do it. Fire her up, see if she's still got a pulse."

Tino slid into the driver's seat, turning the key. The engine rumbled to life, smooth as whiskey on a cold night.

"She purrs," he said, grinning. "Nice work, boss."

I snorted. "Don't call me that."

"But you are, hermano," Marco said from across the bay, tossing a wrench from one hand to the other. "Look at you—Romy Cruzer, businessman. Who woulda thought?"

I shot him a look. "Shut up and get back to work."

He only smirked, but he did as I said, sliding under a Mustang with a socket wrench. The sound of metal on metal filled the space—an honest sound, one that wasn't weighed down by whispered threats or dirty money.

Rafa oversaw the whole thing from the office window, watching like a hawk. We weren't running scams anymore, but old habits died hard. He liked to keep an eye on things, make sure nothing slipped through the cracks.

And my mom? She wasn't here all the time, but she dropped in when she could. Not to micromanage—just to remind me she was proud. Even if she didn't say it outright, I could see it in the way she checked the books, nodded approvingly at the new equipment, smoothed her hand over my shoulder in passing like she needed to make sure I was real.

The shop wasn't perfect. But it was ours.

Legit.

Something I could finally stand behind without the weight of expectation crushing my ribs.

And for a little while, that was enough.

Then I heard it.

A name.

Her name.

At first, it was background noise—just voices bleeding together in the break room, half-muffled by the radio. I wasn't even listening. Not until the syllables hit like a bullet to the spine.

Juliet.

The rag slipped from my hands. My pulse spiked, breath catching in my throat.

I moved before I could think, shoving the door open so hard it banged against the wall.

Marco jolted upright, blinking at me. "Yo, what the hell—"

"What did you just say?" My voice came out too sharp, too ragged.

He exchanged a glance with Uncle Rafa before looking back at me. "Nothing, man. Just—"

"Don't lie to me." My chest was tight, breath coming too fast. "Say her name again."

Silence.

Rafa tried to pull me back, voice low. "Romy—"

I ignored him. My focus stayed locked on Marco, on the way his expression shifted—like he'd stepped on a landmine and was trying to decide if moving would make it worse.

"What are you hiding?" My voice dropped to something dangerous. "What the hell happened to Jules?"

No answer.

And then I saw it.

The flicker of something in Rafa's eyes. A crack in the wall he always kept up.

Doubt.

My heart slammed against my ribs.

She was dead. She was dead.

Buried. Gone. For more than a whole goddamn year.

So why did Rafa look like he was about to be sick?

I took a step back, shaking my head. "You're lying."

"I'm not."

"Then why do you look like that?" My fists clenched. "Tell me the truth."

A muscle ticked in his jaw. "Sit down."

I didn't.

Because in that moment, sitting felt like surrender. And I wasn't ready to surrender—not to this. Not to the idea that maybe, just maybe, I'd spent the last year grieving a girl who wasn't even in the ground.

I stood there, weight shifting like I couldn't find solid ground.

And then Rafa laid it all out.

The deal. The hospital hallway. The war that almost turned that night into a bloodbath.

Montclairs and Cruzers standing across from each

other, fists clenched, eyes filled with a rage too lethal to contain. The walls reeked of antiseptic and tension, the hum of machines barely covering the sound of my father's voice, sharp as a blade.

They made a pact.

No more bloodshed. No more war. No more us.

And the price?

"Juliet Montclair and Romeo Cruzer are never to see each other again."

"By any means necessary."

The words blurred. Hemorrhages. Ruptured organs. Unstable vitals.

Jules slipping away while I was unconscious.

And then, the lie.

That she was gone.

Something inside me buckled. The ground tilted.

I wasn't standing anymore—I was falling.

I sucked in a breath, but it didn't help. My lungs felt too tight, my ribs like they'd been crushed under the weight of something I couldn't name.

"You all lied to me," I whispered, barely recognizing my own voice.

Rafa didn't flinch. His face was carved from stone.

"It was the only way, Romy. The only way to stop the war on us."

I let out a sharp, bitter laugh. "So you let me think she was dead?"

No apology. No hesitation.

Just silence.

I wanted to hit something. Wanted to drive my fist through the closest wall, pick up a wrench and wreck something. Because wasn't that what they'd done to me? They'd wrecked me. Left me stranded in the wreckage of my own grief.

Tino took a step toward me, cautious, like he knew I was about to detonate. "Romy, man, just—"

I shook my head once, sharp. If I let them speak, if I stayed another second, I'd lose my damn mind.

I turned on my heel and walked out.

"Romy—"

I didn't stop. Didn't look back.

Because there was only one place I needed to be.

The driveway was longer than I remembered. All granite and power, edged with those ridiculous manicured hedges that screamed old money and ruthless ambition. The Montclairs had never been subtle about what they were.

I didn't bother knocking.

Didn't wait for an invitation.

I pushed open the door like I had every damn right to be there.

The house smelled the same—like expensive cologne and something colder, sharper. Something that made my teeth clench.

The kind of house that had ghosts.

Victor Montclair stood at the far end of the foyer, hands in his pockets, a shadow cutting against the sterile glow of the chandelier. He watched me like he'd been expecting this moment for a long time.

Like he'd known, even when I didn't, that I'd come for her.

His lips curled, just slightly. "Took you long enough," he said. Like this was a game. Like we were playing by his rules.

I stepped closer, heart punching against my ribs. "Where is she?"

Victor didn't blink. Didn't flinch. Just exhaled slowly, eyes cold, calculating.

"I was beginning to think you'd never show."

I didn't have time for this.

I surged forward, grabbed the lapels of his suit jacket, shoved him against the marble wall. "Where. Is. She."

His hands stayed in his pockets, like I was amusing him. Like I was nothing more than some reckless kid throwing a tantrum in a house that wasn't his.

"You always did have a temper," he murmured, voice smooth as glass. "That's exactly why you were never good enough for her."

My fingers tightened in the fabric. My blood roared. "You think I give a shit about your approval?"

His smirk didn't waver. Didn't crack. He just exhaled slowly, like he had all the time in the world.

"No," he said, voice steady, deliberate. "But I think you still care about my daughter."

And just like that, the ground beneath me wasn't solid anymore.

It was freefall.

Because he wasn't wrong. He knew it. I knew it. And that was exactly why he still held all the cards.

XoXoXo

CHAPTER 22: FIND ME AT THE FINISH LINE

Juliet "Jules" Montclair

France was never the plan.

I told myself that a thousand times.

The engineering program at the Sorbonne was prestigious, competitive—one of the best in the world. It was the kind of place my father approved of, the kind of place that looked good on paper, the kind of place where Montclairs thrived. And, of course, I did.

There wasn't a single class I didn't dominate. I built engines faster, pushed simulations further, saw the mechanics of a machine the way artists saw color. My professors called me brilliant. My classmates called me untouchable. The only girl in a sea of driven, ambitious men, and I never let them forget it.

And yet, no matter how many tests I aced or equations I shattered, there was always something missing. A hum beneath my skin that never quieted, a restless ache that came alive every time I closed my eyes.

Because none of this would have been possible without him.

Without Romy.

I never said his name out loud. Not in this city. Not when the streets smelled different, when the neon signs were in another language, when the weight of my father's world wasn't suffocating me at every turn. But he was there. In the oil beneath my fingernails. In the way I handled a wrench like a second heartbeat. In the way my pulse kicked whenever I heard the low, rumbling growl of an engine that sounded even remotely like his.

At night, when Paris was lit up like a fever dream, I would slip out onto the balcony of my apartment, breathing in the city like it could quiet the storm inside me.

I had everything I'd ever been told to want. A future. A degree that meant something. Freedom, in a way.

And yet—

I still dreamed in gasoline and wildfire.

I still felt him like phantom limbs, like a missing part of me that France could never replace.

I let the world see Juliet Montclair—the prodigy, the engineer, the girl who belonged here.

But when the city hummed with something wilder, something alive, I became someone else.

Not Jules. Not Nyx.

Just Juliet.

Apparently, in France, that was a common name.

The days belonged to Victor Montclair's daughter.

I woke early. Always early.

Pressed shirts, sharp heels clicking against the marble floors of campus, eyes tracking me like I was something delicate, something untouchable. It wasn't admiration. It was expectation. The kind that lived in the rigid tilt of a professor's nod, in the way my name rolled off their tongues like a promise they had made with my father long before I had ever stepped into this world.

I played the part. Sat in the front row. Answered with precision. Buried myself in the mechanics of speed—gear ratios, thermal dynamics, aerodynamics. I understood cars in ways the professors hadn't expected. Understood their heartbeat, their hunger.

I was the only girl in the program, and that fact alone made me a novelty.

The boys flirted. Some were clever, some brilliant. They threw stolen glances across lecture halls, held doors open a second longer, let their hands brush mine when passing notes. Some of them were pretty. Some of them were persistent.

None of them were him.

None of them made my pulse stutter the way he did.

I didn't let myself think about that. About him. About the hands that had once traced my skin like I was something holy, about the way his voice still haunted the spaces between my ribs. About how, even now, when I closed my eyes, I still smelled engine oil and leather and us.

So I worked. I excelled. I made sure there was never a moment of stillness, never an opportunity for my mind to slip into dangerous territory.

But the nights—

The nights were mine.

Juliet wasn't a Montclair. She didn't sit in ivory towers, sipping espresso with heirs to empires. She didn't let the world tell her what she could and couldn't do.

She drove.

The first time I found them—Paris's underground racers—it felt like slipping into something inevitable. Like stepping through a door I hadn't realized had been waiting for me my whole life.

They gathered in the forgotten corners of the city, where neon lights bled into wet pavement, where the scent of burnt rubber clung to the air like a challenge. I showed up in a borrowed car, nothing flashy, nothing that screamed Montclair, and lined up at the start.

They took one look at me and laughed.

Until I left them in the dust.

It was always the same after that. A bet. A thrill.

The moment before the start, when the world narrowed to a single pulse of electricity.

I lived for that moment.

Because for those few, fleeting seconds—when the city blurred, when my heartbeat matched the roar of the engine, when I was faster than the ghosts that chased me—I almost didn't miss him.

Almost.

It started like any other race.

The crowd pressed in around me—strangers in leather jackets and stolen time, cigarette smoke curling in the air, neon reflections stretching across the wet pavement like ghosts. Engines rumbled, a steady, snarling heartbeat beneath the night. Paris had its own rhythm, its own scent, its own unwritten rules. I had learned them all.

I exhaled slow, fingers curling around the wheel, the familiar weight of it grounding me. The car thrummed beneath me, waiting. I scanned the crowd out of habit, looking for threats, for tells, for any sign that the race had already been decided before the light turned green.

And then—

I saw him.

A face half-hidden in the shadows. A profile I had memorized in another lifetime. A ghost.

It wasn't possible. It couldn't be.

But my body knew before my mind did—something inside me tightening, curling into something sharp and breathless. The weight of a year pressed down all at once, suffocating. Romy.

My pulse roared in my ears. My grip on the wheel tightened.

The signal light flickered. The countdown began.

Red.

And suddenly—

The hospital.

White sheets. Cold metal beneath my fingertips. The ache in my ribs like an old wound reopening. The sterile scent of antiseptic, of something deeper, something metallic. Blood.

I remembered the blur of movement, the weight of a body pressing against mine, the sensation of falling—falling—falling—

And then nothing.

The first thing I saw when I woke up was my

father.

Victor Montclair stood at the edge of the hospital room, speaking in low, measured tones. Controlled. Detached. His posture was sharp as a blade, as if he had already turned my near-death into a lesson.

He wasn't alone.

The Cruzers.

They stood just outside the emergency bay, their presence an echo of something unsaid. Raul. Gabriela. Talking in hushed voices. Watching. Waiting.

And then—

A handshake.

A bargain.

And then I heard it.

"Juliet Montclair and Romeo Cruzer are never to see each other again."

"By any means necessary."

My stomach twisted. The sharp inhale of my breath snapped me back into the present.

Yellow.

I clenched my jaw, forcing the memories down, but my hands trembled against the wheel. It was just my mind playing tricks on me.

It had to be.

I looked again.

And I saw him.

Again.

Romy.

Standing on the edge of the crowd, his hands shoved into the pockets of his leather jacket, his gaze tracking the lineup of cars but never seeing me.

Not yet.

I swallowed hard, heart hammering against my ribs. He was here. He was real.

And I remembered.

The note I had left him. The only thing I could leave him.

"If you ever need to run, find me at the finish line."

Green.

The race began.

And for the first time in over a year, I forgot how to breathe.

x o x o x o

CHAPTER 23: ONE LAST RACE

Romeo "Romy" Cruzer

The first time I faced Victor Montclair, I was seventeen, with a bruised ego and stupid enough to think I could win him over.

This time, I wasn't a kid anymore.

The room was heavy with silence. A low fire crackled in the hearth, shadows stretching long over the mahogany floors. Victor's study smelled like expensive cologne, old books, and something herbal—tea, I realized, as he reached for a porcelain teapot and poured two cups. The motion was slow, deliberate, like a man who had all the time in the world.

"I switched from whiskey to tea," he said, not looking at me. "Doctor's orders."

I didn't touch mine. I sat down without waiting for an invitation, my elbows on my knees, fingers laced together to keep them steady.

Victor finally lifted his gaze, exhaling like he'd been waiting for this moment longer than either of us wanted to admit.

"So you found out." His voice was unreadable.

I didn't blink. "Jules is alive."

Victor inhaled slowly, like the words weren't new to him, just inevitable. "Which means you already know why we did what we did."

Jules.

Alive.

The word sat heavy in my chest, pressing against my ribs like a weight I hadn't realized I'd been carrying for a year.

"You lied to me," I said. "To both of us."

Victor took a sip of tea before answering, the edge of his cup tapping against the saucer when he set it down. "You should be thanking me."

I let out a sharp, humorless laugh. "For what? Making my life hell?"

"For keeping you both alive." His voice was even, but there was something behind it, something sharp. "Tell me, Romeo. Do you really think you would've survived if I hadn't intervened?"

The silence stretched. I let it.

"You sent hitmen after me," I said finally, my voice low, controlled.

Victor didn't flinch.

He didn't deny it.

"It was a message," he said, as if that justified everything. "You refused to listen to your father. You refused to listen to me. You were reckless, and you almost got my daughter killed."

My pulse pounded, but I didn't move.

"The race," I said, forcing myself to breathe, to keep my voice level. "She—"

"She was never supposed to be on that track."

Victor's voice was quiet. Not cold. Not cruel. Just... final.

"She went in after you anyway. By the time the first responders pulled you both out, you were barely breathing. You were lucky to make it out at all."

A muscle in my jaw twitched. I clenched my fists under the table.

"Jules?" I forced the word out. "What happened to her?"

Victor exhaled, running a hand over his face. For the first time, he didn't look like the untouchable CEO, the man who'd spent his entire life controlling everything. He just looked tired.

"She survived." His voice was unreadable. "But it took time. A long time. She wasn't the same after that night."

Something twisted in my chest.

"She's happy now," he continued. "Living the life she was meant to. The life she always wanted."

I swallowed the ache, the year of not knowing, of sleepless nights wondering about all the things I could have done differently.

So that she could still be alive.

"I was reckless," I admitted, my voice raw. "I was young, and I thought—"

I shook my head.

"It doesn't matter," I muttered. "I just—I'm sorry.

For all of it."

Victor watched me, expression unreadable.

"I know," he said.

That was the part that caught me off guard.

"I've been keeping tabs on you," he continued, swirling the untouched tea in his glass. "The Cruzers are clean now. The garage, the business—everything. That was your doing, wasn't it?"

I nodded slowly.

"I thought it was about survival," Victor said, studying me. "But now I see it's about her."

I didn't say anything. I didn't have to.

Victor sighed. Then, for the first time, he hesitated.

"When you see her…" His voice softened just enough to be real. "Tell her that everything I did was because I love her."

I nodded once.

Victor reached into his desk, pulled out a crisp piece of paper, and slid it across the polished wood.

An address.

Paris. Sorbonne.

Jules.

I picked up the paper and stood.

Victor didn't say anything else. He just watched me go.

And then I booked a flight to Paris.

Paris smelled like rain and gasoline.

I kept my head down as I stepped out of the airport, the damp air pressing against my skin, heavy with the scent of exhaust and wet pavement. The city glowed—streetlights casting long shadows, headlights cutting through the mist, neon signs blinking in the distance like they were winking at me. I should've gone straight to a hotel, figured out a plan, done something smart.

But I'd never been good at that.

Instead, I found myself moving, my boots scuffing against cobblestone as I followed the GPS to the university. *The Sorbonne.* The name felt foreign in my mouth, too polished, too far from the world we'd come from.

The campus stretched out in front of me, tall windows flickering with low light, casting warm glows onto empty sidewalks. It looked expensive. Old money. The kind of place Jules was always meant to belong. The kind of place that made someone like me feel like an outsider just for breathing the same air.

I didn't belong here.

But I kept walking.

The streets blurred into alleyways, alleys into winding roads, and then—

Engines.

The low growl of a throttle opening up, the sharp crack of a backfire.

I didn't think. Instinct kicked in before logic.

I followed the sound.

The crowd was thick, pressed in tight, bodies radiating heat as people shouted and threw down wads of cash. The air pulsed with bass-heavy music, cigarette smoke curling in the glow of neon. A familiar scene, even an ocean away.

Then I heard it.

Her name.

"Juliet."

My breath hitched.

I turned toward the starting line, heart slamming into my ribs.

And there she was.

Fingers curled around the wheel. But I knew. I knew the way she leaned forward, the way she tapped the clutch just before the signal light flickered, the way her entire body became the car before the race even started.

Jules.

The light turned green.

She was a bullet. A streak of silver and fury.

She tore down the street, the growl of her engine vibrating in my chest. I watched her weave through the other racers like she wasn't even trying—like she was something untouchable, unstoppable.

The way she had always been.

Of course, she won.

The crowd roared as she pulled past the finish line, her tires screeching as she slowed, twisting the wheel with the same reckless precision that used to leave me breathless.

By the time I shoved through the bodies, she was climbing out of the car, helmet under her arm, sweat glistening along her collarbone. Someone handed her a beer, and she took it without looking, the smirk on her lips sharp enough to cut.

I took a step forward—

Then hesitated.

How do you tell someone you're not dead?

How do you tell someone you're sorry?

That you never stopped thinking about them?

Then—

She looked up.

Right at me.

The smirk faded.

And in that one second, the world stopped.

XoXoXo

CHAPTER 24: SMOKE AND GHOSTS

Juliet "Jules" Montclair

There were ghosts in Paris.

Not the kind that clung to forgotten alleyways or flickered beneath gaslight. Not the tragic, romantic ones whispered about in stories.

No, the ghosts I knew had weight.

They smelled like gasoline and regret, left fingerprints on my ribs where they'd pressed too hard, too fast. They carried the taste of blood and metal, of a summer spent burning through asphalt and nights spent convincing myself that loving him hadn't been the worst mistake of my life.

I thought I'd buried this one a year ago.

And yet—

Romy Cruzer.

He was standing there, just past the edge of the crowd, in my city, in my world, looking like he had every damn right to be here. Looking like he hadn't torn through my life like a wildfire and left nothing but embers in his wake.

And the worst part?

He was wearing a shirt. A crisp, button-down, sleeves rolled just enough to show the edge of a tattoo I used to trace with my fingers. For heaven's sake, Romy Cruzer in a formal shirt underneath his jacket.

I wanted to laugh.

I wanted to rip it off him just to prove that underneath, he was still the same reckless boy who kissed me like he didn't care about consequences.

Instead, I swallowed hard.

The roar of my victory was still echoing around me—cheers, congratulations, money changing hands. Someone shoved a bottle into my palm, cold glass pressing against my skin. I barely noticed. Because Romy was here, and for the first time in a long time, I didn't feel like I was winning.

He was watching me. The way he always had. Like I was something he could never quite hold onto, no matter how hard he tried.

Like he was trying to memorize me.

Like he still loved me.

My fingers dug into my palm.

I wanted to run to him. I wanted to turn around and pretend I hadn't seen him.

But I wasn't seventeen anymore.

I didn't run from things.

So I walked straight toward him.

His jaw tightened the closer I got, his hands shoved into the pockets of a leather jacket that had seen better days. It was wrong—seeing him like this, standing under Parisian streetlights instead of bathed in the red glow of brake lights.

He looked different.

Harder. More contained. Like he'd learned how to hold himself together in the year since I last saw him. The boy I had loved was all sharp edges and reckless devotion, a wildfire burning too hot to last. But this version of him carried something heavier in his stance, something quieter. Something that made me wonder just how did he manage to survive when the whole world thought he was dead.

I stopped just short of him, the space between us thick with unsaid things. The crowd still buzzed around us—bets being settled, engines cooling, the air thick with the scent of burning rubber—but none of it mattered. Not when he was looking at me like that.

"Juliet," he said, voice low, rough around the edges.

I let the name linger between us. My father's voice had always curled around it like a leash, something meant to remind me of who I was supposed to be. But with Romy, it was different. It always had been.

"You're alive."

The words tasted foreign in my mouth, like I was testing them for the first time. A statement. A confirmation. A betrayal.

His lips twisted, like he couldn't decide whether to smirk or apologize.

"Yeah," he said. "Seems that way."

I exhaled sharply, shaking my head. "That's it? No Hey Jules, sorry I disappeared off the face of the earth, sorry I let you think I was dead?"

A muscle in his jaw ticked. "Would you have believed me?"

I hated that he was right.

Because if he had called, if he had tried, I would have thought it was a lie. Some last-ditch effort to drag me back into the world I had barely crawled out of. A world that still had its claws in me, no matter how much I pretended otherwise.

The weight of the past year pressed down on me, the ache of it settling into my bones. I had spent months trying to hate him, to erase him, to convince myself that Romy Cruzer was just a chapter I had closed. And yet, here he was, standing in front of me, tearing through my resolve like he always did.

He tilted his head slightly, watching me. "Can we—" He exhaled, running a hand over his jaw, fingers dragging along the stubble there. "Can we walk?"

I should have said no.

I should have turned around, should have let him become a ghost again.

But I didn't.

I nodded.

And just like that, we were in motion, stepping off the edge of the racetrack and into something neither of us were ready for.

We moved through the streets of Paris like ghosts—silent, untethered, caught between past and present. The city pulsed around us, neon lights reflecting in rain-slicked pavement, a late-night saxophone weeping somewhere in the distance. The air smelled like rain, cigarettes, and something indulgent—perfume and espresso and the kind of recklessness found only in foreign cities after midnight.

I had spent a year learning how to be someone else. Someone who didn't flinch at the name *Romy Cruzer*. Someone who didn't wake up gasping, reaching for a boy who was never coming back.

And yet, here we were.

Neither of us spoke at first, letting the city's hum fill the silence, thick as smoke curling between us. I watched him from the corner of my eye—the shift of his shoulders, the way his fingers curled into the pockets of his jacket like he was holding something in.

He looked different. Harder. The boy I had loved had been all sharp edges and reckless devotion, but this version of him carried something heavier, something quieter.

I broke first. "Why now?"

Romy exhaled slowly, rubbing the back of his neck. "Your father."

The words made me stop short. A sharp, involuntary halt, like I had just hit a wall.

My father had built his life out of power and control, of cold negotiations and ruthless precision. He didn't make mistakes, and he sure as hell didn't regret them.

"What about him?" My voice was smooth, a blade wrapped in silk.

Romy turned fully, his hands flexing at his sides. "He told me the truth."

I forced a breath through my teeth. "And what truth is that, exactly?"

His jaw tightened. "That you were alive."

Something inside me cracked. A small, nearly imperceptible thing. But I felt it.

"What?"

Romy's gaze darkened, like the words burned. "They told me you were dead, Jules." He swallowed hard. "My family. They told me you were gone."

I stared at him, the weight of his words pressing against my ribs. Dead. They told him I was dead.

The rage came first, white-hot and blinding. Then the realization.

"He told me the same thing."

Romy stilled.

I let out a hollow laugh, but it didn't sound right, didn't feel real. "My father told me you were dead, Romy." The words felt foreign in my mouth, like something out of a twisted fairytale.

He swore under his breath, his hands running through his hair. He looked at me like he was seeing a ghost. Maybe I was. Maybe we both were.

A year of mourning. A year of thinking he was gone.

A year of him thinking the same about me.

He hesitated. "He told me about everything. About why he did it. About why he lied to you."

The world tilted, just slightly.

He told me about everything.

Not *I found out* or *I figured it out*—but *he told me*. My father, the man who ruled over my life with an iron grip, had chosen to admit something. To *him*.

Something sharp curled in my chest. I folded my arms, a brittle shield against whatever was coming next. "And you believed him?"

Romy's gaze locked onto mine, dark and unreadable. "I think he wanted your forgiveness."

A cold, humorless laugh clawed its way up my throat. "That's rich."

Forgiveness. My forgiveness. As if my father had ever been the kind of man who needed it. As if he hadn't spent my entire life making sure I understood that power meant never having to ask for anything— especially absolution.

Romy looked like he wanted to say more, but he just clenched his jaw. Then, softer, "He said everything he did was because he loves you."

I scoffed, but the words sank deep, wrapping around old wounds and peeling them open like fresh bruises.

I had spent years waiting for my father to love me the way I wanted him to. Waiting for proof that I was more than just a well-executed plan. And yet, even now, standing on a Parisian street with Romy, the weight of his choices pressing against my ribs, I didn't know if I wanted that proof or if I wanted to burn it.

I swallowed hard, pushing the thought away. "And what about you?"

His brow furrowed slightly. "What about me?"

"Why did you come?"

For a second, he didn't answer. His jaw tightened, his gaze flicking away—like he could find the words somewhere in the wet pavement. Then he sighed, shaking his head slightly, like he was trying to shake me off.

"I don't know," he admitted, voice rough. "I just—I needed to see you."

A breath I hadn't realized I was holding slipped past my lips. "So what now?"

He let out a slow exhale, his fingers twitching like he wanted to reach for me. "I don't know." His voice was raw, wrecked.

And maybe that was the only thing that mattered. That after everything, after the lies and the grief and the stolen time—we had still found our way back.

He looked at me, something splintering in his expression. "What do you want, Jules?"

I could have said a thousand things.

I could have said nothing.

But instead, I reached for his hand.

I didn't say *forever.*

I didn't say *never.*

I just said, "Let's figure it out."

And for now, that was enough.

×o×o×o

CHAPTER 25: TILL I DIE

Romeo "Romy" Cruzer

"Let's figure it out."

That wasn't enough.

Not after a year and a half of losing her. Of clawing through hell, of staring at an empty road that was supposed to have her car on it, supposed to have her in it, but didn't.

Not after waking up every morning with my ribs cracked open from the weight of her absence, with her name burning the back of my throat like a cigarette I couldn't put out.

Not after I thought she was dead.

Jules had been my fire, my road flare in the dark, the only person who ever made me believe in something more than just this—a life of stolen cars, whispered threats, and the kind of loyalty that could get you killed.

And she was standing right in front of me, telling me to figure it out.

I let out a breath, slow, deliberate, like I was trying to keep my hands from shaking. Like I was trying not to grab her and make her feel everything I had spent the last eighteen months trying to bury.

"That's not good enough, Jules." My voice came out rough, wrecked. "Not for me."

She stilled, barely breathing. I swore I saw her hands tremble before she curled them into fists.

"Romy—"

"Do you know what it was like?" I cut in, my chest heaving. The city around us felt like it had gone silent, like it was just the two of us and this thing between us, jagged and bleeding. "Do you know what it's like to wake up every day thinking the person you love most in this world is gone?"

Her breath hitched.

"I didn't just lose you, Jules. I lost the only thing that ever made me feel like more than a name people spit on the pavement." My hands clenched at my sides, my pulse hammering. "I tried to move on. I tried to let you go. But I couldn't—I fucking couldn't. Every time I closed my eyes, you were there. In my head. In my heart. In the damn air."

She flinched like the words hit her. And maybe they were supposed to. Maybe she needed to feel it.

"I couldn't even stay in Toronto." The words scraped my throat like gravel. "I left. You know that? I fucking left."

She blinked.

"I couldn't walk those streets without seeing you." My jaw tightened. "I couldn't hear an engine rev without thinking of the way you used to race me just to piss me off. Couldn't pass by the garage without expecting you to be there, leaning against the workbench, telling me my brakes were shit and I'd get myself killed if I didn't let you fix them."

Jules looked down, her breath uneven.

"So I ran. I drove out of that city and kept going.

Ended up in Montreal for a while, then Halifax, then fucking Vancouver. I tried to outrun you, but you were everywhere. In the rearview. In my goddamn pulse. I woke up every day expecting it to hurt less, and it never did."

She swallowed hard, like she was trying to keep herself together.

"I hated you for it," I admitted, voice low. "For making me love you so much it damn near destroyed me."

Silence. A sharp, electric thing stretching between us.

Jules opened her mouth, then hesitated. Like there was too much, like it was stuck in her throat.

And then, quietly, "It destroyed me too."

Something inside me snapped.

"I spent a year hating myself for not saving you." My voice dropped lower, something raw and wrecked seeping in. "I spent a year wondering what I could've done differently. And you know the worst part?"

Jules swallowed, her eyes shining under the streetlights. "What?"

I let out a breath that tasted like gasoline and

heartbreak. "I would've died for you that day. I almost did."

Her face crumpled.

"Romy—"

But I wasn't finished. I couldn't stop. The words had been stuck in my throat for eighteen months, choking me, and now they were coming out in a flood.

"You remember the track that night?" My voice was barely above a whisper, but it carried, heavy with the weight of what we lost. "The smell of burnt rubber. The way the whole place was buzzing, people packed into the stands, waiting for blood."

Jules squeezed her eyes shut, like she could push the memory back down.

I didn't let her.

I saw it like it was happening all over again—the flicker of brake lights, the blur of her taillights, the way she pushed her car to its limits to keep me out of the line of fire.

"A shot rang out."

Jules exhaled sharply, like the sound still lived inside her bones.

"Glass exploded from your rear windshield."

She flinched.

"Jules!" The memory ripped through me, as sharp as the night it happened. "Somehow I managed to connect to the Bluetooth in your car."

I could still hear it—how the static filled my ears, louder than my own pulse.

"Pick up, Montclair. Pick up."

Nothing.

I swallowed hard. She could hear me. But she couldn't respond.

"'Jules, listen to me." My voice cracked, and I didn't even try to hide it. "You need to get out of here.''

Nothing.

"Another bullet whizzed by, missing your driver's side mirror by a hair." My fingers curled into fists. "Goddamn it, Jules! Move it!"

Her taillights flashed like she hesitated.

"'I love you.'" The words were razor blades, slicing their way out of me. "Nothing. I had never said it before. Not like that. Not when I knew what it meant."

Jules sucked in a breath, but I wasn't done.

"I told you I'd love you till I die." I took a step closer, closing the space between us. My voice was quieter now, but no less lethal. "And I fucking meant it."

She shook her head, fast, like she could shake the words off. "Don't. Don't talk about that night."

"Why not?"

Her breathing was uneven now, her shoulders rising and falling like she was trying to hold herself together.

"Because—" She sucked in a sharp breath, then exhaled like it hurt. "Because how do you think I would've felt if you died without even giving me a chance to say it back?"

Her voice cracked, and something inside me did too.

Jules let out a sharp, broken laugh—one that didn't belong on her lips, one that sounded like it had been buried under eighteen months of guilt.

"You think you were the only one who wanted to die that night?" Her hands clenched at her sides, and for the first time, I saw it. The weight she carried. The nights she must've spent haunted by the same goddamn ghosts as me.

She didn't look at me when she spoke again. Her

voice was quieter now, but no less brutal.

"You don't get it, Romy." Her breath shook. "It would've been easier if I had died that night instead of you. Because every single day after that, I had to wake up knowing you weren't there. That I had to keep going, pretending I was fine, when all I wanted to do was disappear with you. You weren't the only one who didn't make it out of that crash—I left a part of myself on that road too."

The words hit like a fist to the ribs.

I thought I had been the only one drowning. But Jules had been there too, just beneath the surface, waiting for the weight to drag her under.

"Do you know how many times I've replayed that night in my head?" She was looking at me now, her eyes fierce, furious. "Over and over again, thinking— what if I'd just said it? What if I could've just fucking said it back? What if you could actually hear me say that?"

Silence stretched between us, thick with everything we had lost, everything we could still lose.

I reached for her then, my fingers brushing her wrist before sliding up to cup her face. Her skin was warm beneath my touch, too warm, like she was burning up from the inside out. She didn't pull away.

"Then say it now." My voice was low, steady, but my hands weren't. "Say it now, Jules."

Her lower lip trembled, but she held my gaze, those storm-cloud eyes searching mine, looking for something—maybe a way out, maybe a way back. Her fingers curled into the fabric of my jacket, like she was bracing herself.

But she didn't say it.

Instead, her mouth opened, then closed, like the words were stuck in her throat, like she was afraid if she let them out, she wouldn't survive it.

I exhaled slowly, my thumb tracing her cheekbone, anchoring her to this moment, to me.

"It's okay." The words came quieter than I meant them to, but they settled between us, weighty, unshakable. "You don't have to."

Jules closed her eyes, her breathing uneven, and when she spoke, it was so quiet I almost didn't hear it.

"Why does it feel like if I say it, I'll lose you again?"

My chest ached. A deep, splintering kind of pain that burrowed into the spaces between my ribs, sharp and unrelenting. Because I didn't have an answer. Because she wasn't wrong.

I had lost her once.

I could lose her again.

But not tonight.

I pulled her closer, our foreheads pressed together, her breath warm against my lips.

"Close your eyes."

She swallowed, her breath shaky. "Why?"

"Just do it."

She hesitated, then obeyed.

And then I kissed her.

Hard. Desperate. Like I was making up for every second we had lost. Like I was trying to carve myself into her bones so she'd never doubt it again.

Jules gasped against my mouth, but she didn't pull away. She kissed me back just as fiercely, her fingers sliding into my hair, nails scraping against my scalp, setting every nerve in my body on fire.

I let out a low groan, tightening my grip on her waist, on her back, on her.

She pressed into me, her body molding against mine like she belonged there, like she had never left. I backed her up against the building wall, my hands running down her spine, gripping her hips, holding onto the only thing that had ever felt real.

"Romy—" Her voice was breathless against my lips, her hands fisting in my jacket, like she was afraid I'd disappear if she let go.

I pulled back just enough to look at her, to memorize the way she looked in this moment— flushed, wrecked, eyes dark with something I didn't dare name.

"You can say it, Jules." My voice was barely a whisper. "Say it now."

She let out a shaky breath, her fingers tracing my jaw, like she was memorizing me too.

And then, finally, finally—

"I'll love you." The words slipped out in a whisper, then again, stronger this time. "I'll love you till I die."

Something in my chest cracked open.

Juliet Montclair had been my first taste of something real.

And I was never letting her go again.

XoXoXo

EPILOGUE:
THE LAST SUMMER I LOVED

Tokyo, 2025

The city lay before them, broad and boundless, a confusion of neon and movement that went on and on, never flagging, never tiring. Tokyo by night was a different animal—wired, raging, pulsating with life that convinced you for an instant that the past was left behind.

But ghosts have a habit of keeping pace.

Jules Montclair's fingers curled over the wheel, the leather smooth under her hold. Outside was the thick smell of rain and gasoline, the asphalt still wet, its color mirroring the frenetic brightness of the city. The drone of engines, the sound of sirens far away, the thud of bass emanating from the bars and open doors—it was music of movement, of possibility.

She let out a breath, rolling her neck, attempting to work out the tension that had settled in the deep crevices of her bones. This city was meant to be a do-over. Somewhere she wasn't Jules Montclair, the girl who left too much unspoken. Here, she was merely a driver, merely a smear of motion slicing through the darkness.

And then another car pulled up alongside hers.

Sleek. Familiar. Deadly in a manner that had nothing to do with velocity.

The tinted window came down.

Romy Cruzer.

He slumped back, one hand hanging over the wheel, the other flipping the radio dial as if he had an eternity to waste. The light from a streetlamp hit the sharp corner of his jaw, the same smirk pulling up the corner of his mouth. The same smirk that had always led to trouble. The same smirk that had almost destroyed them both.

His voice crackled over her speakers, smooth as smoke and just as hard to hold onto.

"Didn't think I'd let you leave me in the dust, did you, Montclair?"

Jules breathed slowly out, rolling her shoulders back, steadying herself against something she wasn't ready to name.

She leaned over and picked up the radio. "Wouldn't dream of it, Cruzer. You hanging in there this time, or am I going to have to hold up for you?"

A low chuckle, sinister and aware. "Cute. Real cute."

She patted the gas, enjoying the purr of the engine as it responded to her fingers. "What's the bet?"

"Winner decides where we sleep tomorrow."

Her breath caught. For only an instant.

Tokyo had been an escape. A space that was between then and now, a city in which nobody recognized them, in which they were not the two kids who'd left devastation wherever they'd been. Here, they were only two people misplaced in the crowd, revolving around each other like planets ready to crash.

This wasn't escape anymore.

They weren't on the run.

They were in pursuit of something else altogether.

A flash of something went across Romy's eyes—heat, resistance, something that tasted more like forever.

"You ready?" he challenged, voice a vow, a question.

Jules' hand cramped on the wheel.

"I was born ready."

The light flipped to green.

They sped ahead.

The city dissolved around them, neon flashing by in a rainbow of reds and blues. Tires brushed against asphalt, engines revved, wind ripped through the open windows, and for an instant, Jules felt it—freedom, weightlessness, the kind of reckless abandon that had always been home.

Through the radio, Romy's voice crackled back in. "You know, I missed this. The thrill. The chase."

Jules grinned, clicking into gear as she slammed a sharp turn. The Tokyo skyline whirled around them. "What, you missed me kicking your butt?"

"Nah." His tone rumbled lower, gritty and

genuine. "Missed you."

The words hit like a gut punch, like a jolt of rollercoaster that dropped unexpectedly—inevitable, thrilling, frightening.

She dared a look at him out the window. He wasn't merely gazing at her—he was looking at her, the way he always did. As if he already knew what she was thinking. As if he was expecting her to tell him the thing she hadn't been able to tell him that night, the thing that had almost cost them both everything.

"Where do we go from here?" she asked, her voice only a little louder than the wind.

Romy breathed out, slow and deliberate, as if he'd already resigned himself to the response.

"Where the road takes us."

The finish line stretched out before them.

They didn't lose speed.

They'd been here before—standing on the brink of something unstoppable, hearts pounding in rhythm with the roar of their engines, knowing that the moment they relaxed, it would be done.

Jules clung to the wheel, heartbeat pounding against her ribs.

Perhaps for the first time, it didn't matter if they won.

Perhaps it never had.

Because this wasn't just about the win.

It was about all the stolen moments, all the crazy choices, every time they had picked each other despite being wrong.

It was about the fact that they had lived.

Jules had spent so long believing love was a losing game. That it was designed to end in tragedy, in wreckage, in the sort of heartbreak you never actually managed to walk away from.

But Romy had never played by the rules.

And perhaps, just perhaps, neither had she.

The city lay before them, endless and waiting.

They didn't slow down.

Because this?

This wasn't the end.

This was just the beginning.

"For never was a story of more might and heat—than this of Jules and her Romy, in Tokyo's streets."

THE END

ABOUT THE AUTHOR

Kathy Winslower is a gifted storyteller with a passion for weaving tales of love, resilience, and triumph. With her captivating narratives and richly drawn characters, she takes readers on unforgettable journeys that explore the depths of human emotions and the power of love to transform lives.

Born with an insatiable curiosity and a love for words, Kathy began her writing journey at a young age, filling countless notebooks with her imaginative stories. As she grew older, her passion for storytelling only deepened, leading her to pursue a career as a novelist.

Drawing inspiration from her own experiences and the world around her, Kathy's writing is characterized by its heartfelt authenticity and emotional depth. She skillfully delves into the complexities of relationships, capturing the raw and tender moments that shape her characters' lives.

When she's not immersed in her writing, Kathy can be found exploring nature, seeking inspiration from the beauty of the world around her. She believes that every moment holds the potential for a story, and it is her mission to capture those moments and share them with her reader.

www.ingramcontent.com/pod-product-compliance
Lightning Source LLC
Chambersburg PA
CBHW030535190726
48283CB00006B/1921